GOODNIGHT SWEETHEART

GOODNIGHT SWEETHEART

THE SPARROW DIARIES

Micheál Jacob

BASED ON THE BBC TELEVISION SERIES CREATED BY
LAURENCE MARKS & MAURICE GRAN

Published by BBC Books
a division of BBC Worldwide Limited
Woodlands, 80 Wood Lane
London W12 OTT

First published 1996
© Alomo/Pearson Television Company and Micheál Jacob 1996

ISBN: 0563 38786 6

Designed by Hammond Hammond
Illustrations by Graham Redfern

Set in Stemple Schneidler and Futura

Printed by Martins the Printers Ltd, Berwick-upon-Tweed
Bound by Hunter & Foulis Ltd, Edinburgh
Cover printed by Lawrence Allen Ltd, Weston-super-Mare

As the immortal Al Bowlly sang,
'Love is the sweetest thing'.

Gary Sparrow

OCTOBER 1994

.MONDAY 3.

Mrs Edgar, Laurence Street. Video problem.
Ms James, Grafton Road. No picture.

.TUESDAY 4.

Dr Singh, Charles Street. Dish.

.WEDNESDAY 5.

Birthday!!! Thirty-two today!!! Sod it!!!

.THURSDAY 6.

Mr Wells, Hugh Gaitskell House. Nothing coming through.

.FRIDAY 7.

Last night I met a miserable old git, a bald policeman, and the most beautiful girl in the world. Last night I saved the life of the miserable old git, taught the bald policeman 'Your Song', and fell in love with the most beautiful girl in the world. And I can't tell anybody, because they all live in 1940. In 1940!

I've written it down, but I still can't believe it. It's insane. Me, Gary Sparrow, a television repair man with a small starter home and an upwardly-mobile wife, a time traveller!

Why me? And is it true? Am I having some kind of breakdown? But how can I be, when the lipstick was on my cheek? I need to think about it, write it all out, see if it makes sense.

SATURDAY 8.

Peace at last, a corner of the Dun Cow, a pint, and I can try and work this all out. Maybe if I describe it, then I'll know it was a fantasy. I mean, I'm not Dr Who!

Okay. I had a call to go to Hugh Gaitskell House somewhere round Columbia Road. I couldn't find it in the *A to Z*, the mobile wasn't working, and I asked a policeman for directions. I walked down Duckett's Passage, saw a pub, and went in to ask the way.

The barmaid was wearing 1940s gear. So I thought – this has to be a theme pub. She didn't know Hugh Gaitskell House, and neither did her father, the grumpiest old git I've ever met. He was 1940s as well.

When I asked for directions, he gave me all this stuff about careless talk

PC Deadman points me towards the strangest experience of my life

costing lives. And when I wondered why the pub was full of old codgers, he said the young men had taken the King's shilling. I couldn't resist a crack about the King's gas going out, which went down a bundle. I thought the old sod was going to nut me. Honestly!

Then he wanted to know why I wasn't in uniform. So I thought I'd enter into the spirit of the thing and come over all mysterious – it seemed the only way to get a drink.

Naturally they didn't do lager, and the barmaid said they were only serving halves – at threepence three farthings.

They seemed like bloody good actors. It was only when she rang the money up on the till that I began to wonder what was going

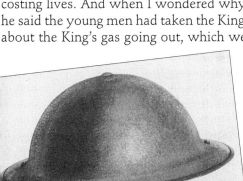

"Keep it under your hat!"

on. Threepence three farthings, it said. So I went outside, and that was when I realized – all the windows had tape over them. There was an anti-aircraft gun at the top of the street. There was a barrage balloon flying overhead. The street-lamps were gas. There was a sign pointing to an air-raid shelter.

Then the copper who had given me directions came down the street, naturally carrying a gas mask, and I asked if the whole street was on the theme lark. He looked at me as if I was mad. I said he'd given me directions not half an hour before. He looked as if I was even madder. 'Half an hour ago,' he said, 'I was doing a bandaging demonstration for the ARP in the Christadelphian Hall. Standing room only, though that might have been the appeal of the rock cakes . . . '

It was then I was sure it was a dream. What else could it be? Would I get my leg over the barmaid? Or would she turn into Aunty Enid as they usually do? Why do they?

So I went for it. After all, you can do anything you want in a dream.

There was a bit of trouble when I offered a cheque for my drink and

Asking for a lager in the Royal Oak didn't improve Eric's temper.
He wasn't too keen on 'My Way' either

took out my birthday present, a rather nice Mont Blanc pen Yvonne gave me. The copper, whose name seemed to be Reg, and the old sod, who was Eric, started having orgasms over it. Then Eric saw it had 'Made in Germany' written on it. And the fun started. Eric wanted Reg to arrest me as a spy and demanded to know where I'd got the pen. For some reason I said America. The barmaid, who turned out to be Eric's daughter, Phoebe, told him not to be silly, and he sent her into the kitchen to get his tea. God, if I tried that on Yvonne . . . Anyway, Eric and Reg cooked up this ludicrous test. Eric scribbled away, then gave me a bit of paper to read. It said: Worcestershire beat Warwickshire by ten wickets. I had to read it aloud.

The test seemed just as mad as anything else, until Reg explained that Germans couldn't pronounce their Ws, so I must be true blue. He shook my hand. Eric couldn't quite apologize, and was still moaning on about money. He and Reg got into a bidding war for the Mont Blanc, which I ended up selling for four shillings and eightpence. Four and eight! 24p!

When I said it cost over £30, Reg had hysterics. Still, what does anything matter in a dream?

So I went over to the piano and started fiddling around with 'Your Song', I don't know why. Phoebe came over for a chat – the leg-over possibilities were looking good, if only Aunty Enid would stay out of the picture.

She asked if I'd learned it in America, so I said I'd written it. And lots of others. I tried a bit of 'My Way', but Eric told me to stop because it was defeatist.

When Phoebe asked me what I did, and I said I was a television repair man, she came over all sympathetic. Times must be hard, with no television since the beginning of the war. So I told her I was now a radar technician, which meant nothing to her. I pretended it was secret war work, and she was definitely impressed.

I discovered she was married, but her husband was away in the army, that she liked going out . . . and then the world fell in. There was an air-raid siren, a huge explosion, and Eric started shouting that everyone should go into the cellar. That was when I wanted to wake up, given my claustrophobia. But I passed out instead.

When I woke up I was sure I was at home. I just couldn't remember

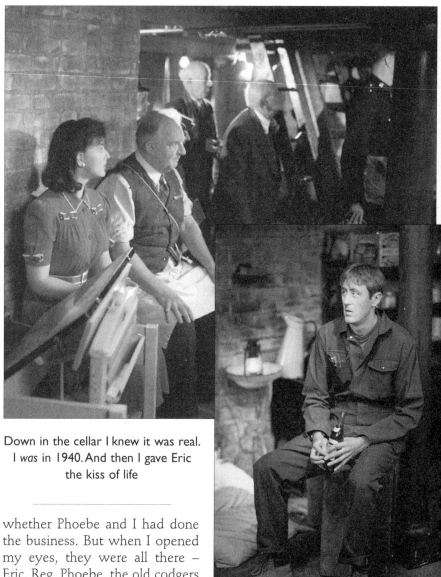

Down in the cellar I knew it was real.
I *was* in 1940. And then I gave Eric
the kiss of life

whether Phoebe and I had done the business. But when I opened my eyes, they were all there – Eric, Reg, Phoebe, the old codgers . . . what a nightmare!

Phoebe, bless her, gave me a slug of brandy. Eric, of course, wanted me to pay for it. Reg suggested a singsong to keep spirits up, and Phoebe said that I wrote songs.

So there I was, in the middle of an air-raid, teaching people who may or may not be figments of my imagination, an early hit by Elton John. Talk about weird! Still, they learned it all right, and with another slug of brandy

I was feeling fine until Eric insisted on going up to get the till-tray. Though who would want to go out in an air-raid to nick a few quid boggles the imagination.

The silly old sod had just got upstairs when there was another explosion. I didn't think. I just rushed up after him and gave him the kiss of life. Reg didn't help. He thought I was snogging Eric instead of trying to save him, and started pulling me off.

By the time Phoebe arrived, Eric was breathing again. Reg said that what I'd done was brilliantly resourceful but not very manly. Phoebe looked at me like I was a hero, which I suppose I was. Am.

She walked me to the bottom of the alley, and dropped a hint about going dancing. Then she kissed my cheek and I went home.

Of course, Yvonne was going spare wondering what had happened. God help me, I tried to tell her the truth. Well, some of the truth, leaving out the 1940s and the bomb. Though I pretended it was a theme pub, which didn't seem too much of a lie. She said a real Yvonne line – 'You don't have to lie to me Gary, I'm not your mother'. And of course, it seemed totally incredible. Until, that was, I looked in the bathroom mirror, and saw Phoebe's lipstick on my cheek.

Phew. I have never written so much in my life. I'll just make the first couple of pages look like a work diary in case Yvonne finds this.

Writing it all down makes me feel better. It almost makes sense.

.SUNDAY 9.

No it doesn't, it makes no sense at all. Perhaps I should see a doctor?

.MONDAY 10.

Keep reading over what I've written and thinking about it. And about Phoebe.

No Gary, keep things simple. If it wasn't a dream then it was a once-in-a-lifetime experience. I'll hide this diary, and maybe look at it once a year.

.TUESDAY 11.

I can't do proper dancing. Would Phoebe mind? I've got to talk to somebody, but who?

.WEDNESDAY 12.

If I can't talk to anyone, at least I can talk to you, dear diary. Why haven't I got any friends? Why does Yvonne keep reminding me that I don't have any friends? Must remember to buy dinner on the way home. Oh, and a new suit.

.LATER.

What a strange night. Yvonne gave me a hard time about buying kidneys for dinner. She spouted some psycho-garbage about me buying them because they look like testicles and I'm punishing her because she makes me do the cooking. Me, Mr New Man. She binned them.

Then she did the suit stuff. I mean, it's a promotion interview, so what? If I get the job, it'll be because of my technical know-how and my innate charisma, not my gentlemen's apparel. She gave me more punishment stuff, about how she's the assistant deputy personnel manager, and I just want to make her look bad. Working for the same company is a bad idea. On the other hand, if we didn't, I wouldn't be living in a boxy little starter home in Cricklewood with a woman who looks a bit like Marilyn Monroe.

I couldn't tell her I'd spent the suit money on a couple of books about the war. And a few tapes. So I told her that the omelettes we were eating represented six weeks' egg ration, fried in a week's worth of butter, and filled with approximately a month's cheese ration. For some reason, she seemed unimpressed.

I played her a bit of Al Bowlly, told her I'd heard him in the theme pub. She said she'd like to go some time, but I told her I wouldn't be able to find it again in the blackout.

When she went off to her psycho-garbage tutorial, I started channel-hopping on the radio. Hearing Churchill gave me a turn, until I realized it was a documentary. Then I found a phone-in, and, would you believe, it was about strange experiences. I just had to call, even if the presenter was called Marty Harty. What a stupid name! I was sure I wouldn't get through but of course I did, first time. They

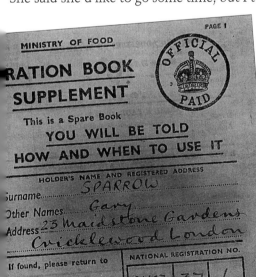

wanted to know what I was called, and I said the first thing that came into my head – Angelo Garibaldi. Well, if someone's called Marty Harty, Angelo Garibaldi sounds quite normal.

I was just telling Marty about my adventure when they cut me off, and

Yvonne gives me a hard time in the kitchen – but she can be stroppy all over the house

I could hear Marty saying that I'd won the Loony of the Week award. Bloody cheek!

Then the doorbell rang. It was Ron, that printer bloke I met at my appalling birthday party, husband of Yvonne's best friend Stella. We had a good chat at the party, about rites of passage and the plight of man in the 1990s. Deep stuff after a few pints. Ron hadn't met Yvonne before, and he summed her up rather neatly, I thought – 'Nice, tight little bum and a bit of a madam'. I wish I had a way with words.

And there he was on the doorstep in a painter's smock and calling me Angelo.

Naturally, I pretended I'd been winding Marty up, but Ron kept nagging away at it, even after we'd got over the misunderstanding of him asking for a little Ricard, me saying I had 'Good Golly Miss Molly' on a compilation album, and him explaining it was a drink. Which of course I knew.

Ron talks funny. It's not just the Liverpool accent, but the way he says things. He sat there smiling at me, and said: 'Did you really wander through some time warp and find yourself in a war-torn yesteryear? I mean, to boldly quote Captain Kirk, it's the final frontier, the ultimate romance.'

I wanted to talk to him, to a person rather than to myself in this diary, but I just didn't know whether or not to trust him. Would he believe me? Would he be like Marty? Would he have me locked up?

So we talked about who we'd like to meet if we could go back in time. Ron said he'd like to meet George Best. I said it was possible to meet him now for the price of a drink, but Ron meant George in his prime, practising his silky skills, and all that.

I said I would like to meet Marilyn Monroe, attracted as I am by her mixture of vulnerability and sexual knowingness, always a killer in women.

Then we got philosophical, which really helped. He may be a strange fat man from Liverpool, but he has a mind.

Ron said everything depended on whether time was a straight road or a winding river. If it was a river, then you could get off the boat and hike back to the bit of the river from before you were born. Then he pointed out that 50 000 people go missing every year, and where do they go? Where are they?

I couldn't answer that. But it makes you think. Perhaps it explains Lord Lucan.

It's 10.15 – Yvonne will be back soon. Time to stop.

.THURSDAY 13.

Perhaps if I say I'm involved in secret radar research with the Americans I'll be able to stop Eric being so bloody suspicious?

.SATURDAY 15.

Bad day, yesterday. But what a night!

Went for the interview – it was crap. Let's be honest – I was crap.

As soon as I walked in and saw three escapees from Burton's window display, I knew I was in trouble. The first question was whether I thought jeans and trainers were suitable apparel for an aspiring manager. Naturally I said that the imposition of anachronistic dress codes is one of the running sores infecting the body of British industrial relations.

Actually, I didn't. What I really said was I only had the one suit, and the cat had been sick on it. They didn't laugh. Bad sign. After that they asked me a few more questions out of politeness, didn't listen to the answers, and threw me out. I could hear them laughing when I shut the door.

Of course, the blonde bomber gave me hell about it, and then she stabbed me in the back. I was popping down to the off licence, forgot my wallet, and came back into the room just in time to hear Yvonne telling Stella on the phone that I hadn't got the job. After she'd sworn to me that she didn't know. Cow!

So I didn't go to the off licence. I didn't really mean to go anywhere, but I saw this flea-market, wandered in, and there was a woman selling 1940s gear. She had a suit someone died in, and a pair of shoes that almost fitted.

So I bought them.

Then I got in the van, drove to Duckett's Passage, changed in the back, walked down the alley and . . . Bingo! There was the barrage balloon, there was the ack-ack gun, there was the Royal Oak, and there was Phoebe! And, of course, bloody Eric. Honestly, you wouldn't think I'd saved his life. And you wouldn't think I'd brought him and Phoebe a priceless present –

Me looking good in my 1940s outfit, even if I say so myself

four bananas. He accused me of being a spiv, so I went into my secret contacts with the Americans story. That shut him up.

I wanted to get Phoebe on her own, but the pub was almost empty, and Eric was ear-wigging, so I asked her straight out if she wanted to go dancing. Eric nearly blew a gasket. What would have happened if Phoebe's mum had gone dancing when he was up to his neck in muck and bullets? Phoebe shut him up beautifully, by telling him that her mum used to be a regular at tea dances up the Royal. I asked Phoebe how old she was. She said twenty-five. I said it seemed that she was old enough to make up her own mind. So we went dancing.

Damn! Promised Yvonne we'd go shopping, so I'd better stop now. And, after last night . . . Phoebe, Phoebe, Phoebe, Phoebe, Phoebe, Phoebe, Phoebe – it looks so good!

.SUNDAY 16.

How now, Dun Cow? The landlord just asked what I was writing. Science fiction, I told him. There was no need for him to say I looked like an anorak, just because I happened to be wearing one.

And I still ache! My feet! My eye!

So we went dancing, and it was great, though if we do it again I'm going to have to take lessons, and find some shoes that fit. I thought I was doing really well with my own version of the jitterbug, but it turned out they were playing a foxtrot, and Phoebe wasn't amused. I told her it was the Shake, something I'd picked up in Hollywood when I was working there writing songs. She said it seemed more like St Vitus's Dance; or was it fleas?

The shoes were giving me gyp, so I said I'd crashed doing 75 in the Indianapolis 500, and woke up in hospital with both legs in traction. I could walk okay, it was only dancing that was a problem. I don't think she believed me, particularly when I said slow dances were all right. And her a married woman!

Phoebe is stunned when I jitterbug instead of doing the foxtrot

I try to give Phoebe some advice about smoking. She thinks I am mad

"You can always trust CRAVEN 'A' quality! They are so smooth and kind to your throat"

I've got so much to learn about her. For instance, she drinks gin and It. And she smokes, although she has to be a lady in front of her father.

'Smoking's bad for your health,' I told her. She looked at me as if I was mad. 'Mark my words,' I said, 'they'll put health warnings on the packets one day.' 'Naah,' said Phoebe. 'Anyway, they're good for your nerves, aren't they? And there's no point worrying about a cough carrying you off when a bomb could land on top of you any second.' I couldn't really argue with that.

We talked about her husband, Donald, who used to work in the custard powder factory, volunteered for the army, and sounded safely out of the way in Africa. She made him seem like a quiet, gentle soul. Then we talked about me. Phoebe wanted to know if I was involved with anyone. I told her the woman I'd marry hadn't even been born, but she kept pressing, so I had to admit there was a girl in America. Phoebe wanted to know her name and I had one of those total blanks. I could hardly say Yvonne. So I said Marilyn, Marilyn Monroe. Phoebe thought it sounded like one of those film star names, bless her. If she lives through the war, she'll certainly have a shock.

So, finally, we had a slow dance, and I smelled her hair and held her close and forgot about my feet. It was magic.

Then I walked her home, serenading her with a verse or two of 'On the Street Where You Live'. I was just getting ready for a goodnight kiss when, wham! Donald, who is unexpectedly home on leave, opens the pub door, jumps on me and gives me a black eye. He's not quiet and gentle – he's a gorilla!

Of course, Yvonne wanted to know what had happened. So I went back to the theme-pub story and said I'd fallen down the trap-door when they asked me to help behind the bar. If she hadn't been feeling guilty, I'd never have got away with it. But she was feeling guilty, and wanted to make it up to me and apologize, and one thing led to another. When she asked me to do what I do best, I told her I wasn't erecting a satellite dish at that time of night. But she had something else in mind, and then I started feeling guilty myself. Life is so difficult.

.MONDAY 17.

Forgot to ask Phoebe how long Donald was staying for. Damn. Must see if I can find a book to discover how long soldiers got for leave in the 1940s.

.TUESDAY 18.

Should I talk to Ron? He seems like the only person who'd believe me, but he's married to Yvonne's best friend. And I'm sure he's the sort of guy who rambles in his sleep. But then, who would believe him?

.WEDNESDAY 19.

Going quietly mad. If I see one more satellite dish, I'll scream. If I meet one more punter who can't tune the video, I'll double scream.

Yvonne seems to have calmed down over the job thing. There's nothing like guilt! Not that I play on it, of course, just mention it from time to time.

Got some good new books about the

Researching the war is useful for all sorts of reasons, not least avoiding the bombing raids

war, a brilliant one with lists of dates. I tried reading some to Yvonne, but she didn't seem to be taking it in. Women, eh? Bet Phoebe would have been interested.

Why did I spin Phoebe all that stuff about America and songwriting? Do I need to ask myself that? God, you're despicable sometimes, Gary Sparrow. But I've always felt that's what I should have been, the great singer/songwriter, the great footballer, the great blues man. It's only fate that stopped me.

Wonder if Donald's gone back yet? He wouldn't have more than a week's leave, would he? I'll give it ten days to be on the safe side. Boy, can he punch! Of course, I'd have laid him out, but I didn't want to upset Phoebe.

Dream on, Gary, as Yvonne would say..

.MONDAY 24.

He must have gone by now, but I'll give it a day or two to be sure.

.WEDNESDAY 26.

Phoned in sick. Mr Jackson not happy. And I'm in love, still in love, madly in love! But I'm in trouble again. This is serious – how can I lead two lives? But it's so exciting!

Yvonne came home when I was staring out the window. I told her I thought I'd heard a Spitfire, but it was only a plane from the flying school. She didn't seem to notice, but she looked at me oddly when I said it was a good night for Jerry to come over. She said we don't know anyone called Jerry.

In fact, she was more concerned about her sister's new baby – the blessed Alison has finally given birth, I'm sure without any assistance from Craig who makes Michael Barrymore look like Mike Tyson. We're godparents, of course. She was all set for us to visit.

Then she had a go at me about spending a mere £120 on a set of books which list every air-raid there ever was, plus other wartime highlights. Why couldn't she see they were a bargain? I told her I'd failed the interview because the only hobbies I could come up with were blues, snooker and watching television, and I thought a detailed study of the Second World War would make me a more interesting person. Yvonne said that fretwork was cheaper. Cow!

I was leafing through the 1940s book when I saw that in this very week Mr Churchill and President Roosevelt concluded a secret arms deal. Then I read something that really churned me up: Enemy action was considerably greater than of late on October 25. Heavy bombing started

The East End gets a pasting from the Luftwaffe. At least I was able to take Phoebe to a safe place

unusually early in the evening over the East End of London. That's today! Or rather, it was yesterday. But I had to do something. So I told Yvonne I'd left my best circuit tester in Holborn, asked her to give my love to Alison, and rushed off.

There's something deeply undignified about a man with very long legs changing in the back of a small van. I'm beginning to wish I was Clark Kent. But I managed it and went straight down Duckett's Passage. Good old Duckett's Passage, my gateway to heaven.

I still wasn't sure about the Donald situation, but I thought if he was still around, I could at least warn Phoebe about the raid, so I looked up the number of the pub and tried to make a call from the phone box round the corner.

I could hear somebody answering, but they couldn't hear me, until Reg came by and told me about pressing Button A for them to hear me, and pressing Button B to get my pennies back. It's another world.

Phoebe answered, which was great, and said that Donald had gone back, which was marvellous. About ten seconds later I was in the pub. I told her I couldn't stay long, but that my secret sources knew there was going to be some heavy bombing and she should either get down the underground or, even better, go to the West End.

Eric started arguing the toss as usual, and then a bloke I'd never seen before got involved. He was wearing a blue uniform, and turned out to be an ARP warden. To be frank, I didn't like his tone. He seemed to think that the ARP would know if there was going to be any bombing. Prat!

The station mistress gives us a hard time. We're rescued by a friendly wartime spiv

Bloody Eric came up with the theory that I was spinning Phoebe a yarn just to get her to go out with me, which was the last thing I needed. I lost my rag a bit, and Phoebe could tell I was really serious, because she took off her pinny and came with me.

'Come on,' I said, 'I'll see you to the nearest bus stop.' Phoebe looked horrified . . . 'You don't think I'm going up West on my own? I've only ever been up West three times in my life, and if you don't come with me . . .'

I hadn't reckoned on this. 'But,' I blurted, 'Yvonne's expecting me back . . .' 'And who's Yvonne when she's at home?' Phoebe wanted to know. I stammered a bit, tried to think of any name other than Sparrow. 'Yvonne Goolagong, my controller,' I said.

Telling Phoebe I wouldn't be long, I rushed back up the passage to the call box, but one side only took cards, and the other side had been vandalized. Then Reg appeared, which I didn't have time to think about then, but I've been thinking about a lot since.

He said something about his granddad. Which means the new Reg must be descended from the old Reg.

But why are they called Deadman? Is the new Reg the reason I got back to the past? Is he a kind of gate-keeper? Did my mind summon him up, or does he really exist? I must think about it more. But I've got to get this all down before Yvonne gets home, then shove the diary in the van with the suit as usual.

We got a bus to Bethnal Green, but that was full, so a copper told us to get a train down the line, and we got off at Holborn, which was mobbed too. I said to Phoebe it was worse than Harrods' sale, and she wanted to know what a Harrod was.

It was weird actually to be there, to be part of

Phoebe says she'll do anything for a bar of chocolate. Pity we're in a public shelter!

something I'd just read about or seen flashes of on some of the videos I've been buying. Somehow, the Royal Oak feels more normal, probably because it's a pub.

But the tube trains were different, and the tube smelt different; there was a really strong niff around the station – a bit like a charity shop, I suppose, only worse. I guess dry cleaners weren't a priority in the war. It was all a bit insanitary really, though Phoebe didn't seem to notice.

I was looking round for somewhere to sit when this jobsworth station mistress demanded to see our tickets. I showed her the tube tickets, but she said she meant a shelter ticket, and where had I been? Phoebe, who's great at standing up for me, snapped that I'd been in America, but had come back here to do my bit. Mrs Jobsworth, wondering what I was doing hiding down the tube in that case, went off, sniggering.

Phoebe said we might as well go home, and we were arguing about it when a dapper old bloke hopped off a bunk and said he'd noticed my wife and I were in a small predicament. I said Phoebe wasn't my wife. She kicked me, quite hard.

The dapper old bloke brushed all that aside, and said he might be able

to oblige me with two shelter tickets – in the upper circle. Gosh, I thought, a spiv! 'You're a spiv,' I said before I could stop myself, but the dapper old bloke didn't seem to mind, though he did make a bit of a song and dance about how much to charge, pointing out that the evening's entertainment was going to be by the Great Alfonso, the most sought-after accordionist on the Central Line. In the end, he asked ten shillings, whistled for his mate on the next bunk, and left us to get up to our own devices.

Phoebe bounced up and down a bit, and seemed happy. I thought I'd tease her by saying that I always fancy a bar of chocolate when I'm down the tube. She said she'd do anything for a bar of chocolate, then blushed.

I whipped out a large-sized fruit-and-nut, which I said I'd got at the American Embassy and asked her what she'd do for it. She wondered what I had in mind, but I got a bit shy and said I'd only been joking. I was amazed when she called me a sauce-box and gave me a smacker on the cheek.

Then I realized that everyone was staring at us, well, not at us exactly, but at the chocolate. They looked a bit like a lynch mob, so I gave Phoebe some, then handed the rest out, leaving none for me. People ignored us after that.

Oh, no! Yvonne will be home soon, and I haven't even got to the good bit yet. Plus I won't be able to find any more time till Saturday. Bollocks. And I need to work out how to talk to Ron.

. SATURDAY 29 .

Still haven't worked out how to talk to Ron. I guess I'm just going to have to take a chance, otherwise it's goodbye to heaven.

Anyway, back to the shelter, back to the war, back to Phoebe. There was a pregnant woman who I made sure got a bit of chocolate, and she seemed very grateful. It went down well with Phoebe, too.

So Phoebe and I started to chat. I wanted to find out everything about her. And, of course, by asking about her, it stopped her asking about me, but she believes whatever I say, and it's wonderful. Not that she believes lies, but that she believes in me. Yvonne thinks the way to get me to do things is to nag and make suggestions and push me in a direction I don't necessarily want to go. It's her agenda. Phoebe just thinks I'm great. She's so sweet, so innocent, well, innocent in some ways, very knowing in others. It's a wonderful mixture.

Obviously we talked about Donald. It sounds as if she gave him a right earful about trust in marriage, and about soldiers taking advantage of the fact that out East you can buy dirty pictures and men can go to, as she said, 'places' . . . That's what I mean about innocent. 'Houses of ill-repute,' I suggested. 'Knocking shops,' she said. I said you couldn't blame soldiers far away from home, but Phoebe wasn't having any of it.

'We stood in St Saviour's and both made vows,' she said. 'What was the point if we didn't mean to keep them? Otherwise, how's a marriage supposed to survive?'

I tried not to look too disappointed. But Donald apologized to her. He said he should have realized that Phoebe and I were just friends, and he believed her when she said I was a perfect gentleman.

This would have been our first kiss, until the Great Alfonso and childbirth got in the way

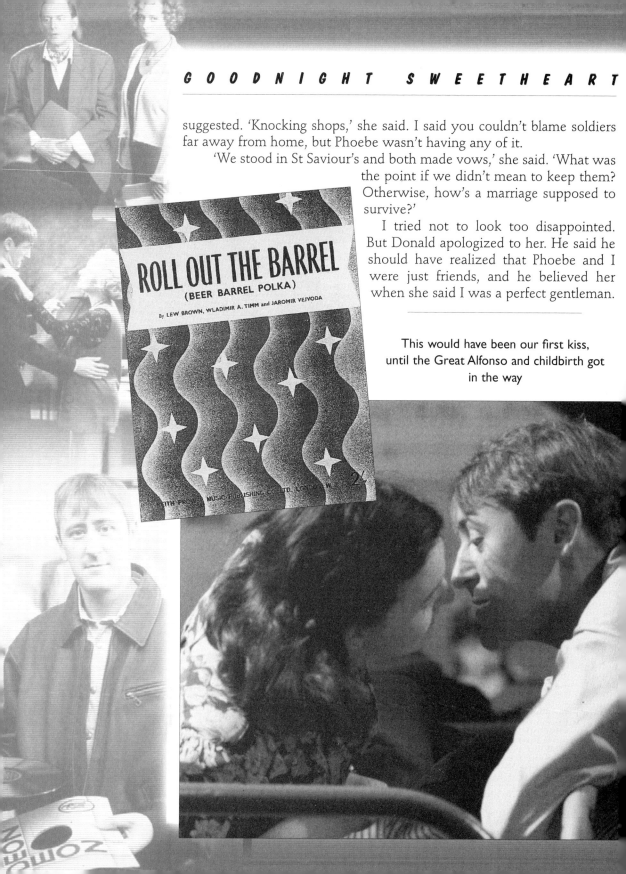

ROLL OUT THE BARREL
(BEER BARREL POLKA)

By LEW BROWN, WLADIMIR A. TIMM and JAROMIR VEJVODA

This didn't seem like very good news, but I agreed that I would be a perfect gentleman if I had to be. Her skin smelled fresh, like springtime.

She amazed me by saying that she only married Donald because she didn't want to spend the rest of her life looking after Eric, and that she didn't really love him – at least not like love in the pictures.

I told her that things would be different after the war and that women would want to do as they pleased, not what they were told. People wouldn't have to stay married if they didn't want to, divorce would be no big deal. People would just live to-gether without being married, they'd have

children, and no one would give a damn. Phoebe looked at me really pityingly. 'You and your imagination', she said.

I started to sing her a bit of 'Imagine', but she shushed me because people were looking. She said she preferred the song I'd sung her earlier, another little composition of mine called 'Yesterday'.

I looked at her, she looked at me, and suddenly there was no one else there at all. I knew that I could take her in my arms and that everything would be perfect for ever. Then the Great Alfonso struck up with 'Roll Out the Barrel' and everyone, including Phoebe, joined in. I didn't. I sulked.

After Alfonso finally shut up, Phoebe nodded off. She'd said she'd been averaging about four hours sleep a night since the Blitz started, so I couldn't really blame her, particularly as the moment had gone.

So I lay on my bunk thinking of what to tell Yvonne. How about I was out all night because the van broke down and my AA membership's lapsed? But she'd ask why I hadn't phoned. How about I got locked into the building where my circuit tester was? But she'd ask why I hadn't phoned.

I'd decided to tell her that I'd spent the night in Holborn station sheltering from the Blitz when the pregnant woman started moaning and screaming, and Phoebe woke up. I tried shouting for a doctor, but that didn't do any good, so I grabbed the woman and told her she'd feel better standing up. She didn't seem to want to take my advice, even though Phoebe told her I knew what I was doing because I'd lived in America.

Then she started hyperventilating, so I grabbed a paper bag and put it over her mouth until her breathing got back to normal. She stopped having hysterics, but she was still screaming in pain – obviously a bad contraction.

I told her to breathe with the pain, and to pant when it got really bad.

Phoebe was a bit suspicious, but I told her I knew about having babies from watching *thirtysomething*. Finally, a nurse arrived and took over.

Then word came that the all-clear had sounded, so I took Phoebe home.

Thank God the Royal Oak was okay, but the area had taken a real battering. For some reason, there was a piano standing in the street, and some poor sod was pushing a pram full of clothes to God knows where. A tea wagon was catering to a group of firemen. The air smelled of smoke and burning, but Phoebe wasn't worrying about the local colour. She was worried about her dad.

I followed her into the pub, to be confronted by two blokes in raincoats and trilbies, one of them smoking a pipe. They were straight out of those 1940s and 1950s movies, and I knew they were coppers. What I didn't know was that they were about to finger my collar. Old Judas Eric pointed them in my direction, while Manny the ARP man looked happy.

The pipe man, who turned out to be called Detective Inspector Howard, asked for my identity card. In a convincing display of *je ne sais quoi* (or is it *sang-froid*?), I patted my pockets and told him I'd left my papers at home. It seemed like no big deal, until Manny pushed forward and suggested that my home was in Berlin.

It was then Howard showed me his ID, and introduced his colleague Detective Sergeant Martin.

My little joke about them coming from the Serious Cliché Squad went down like the proverbial, and they hustled me out to a black Wolseley (another serious cliché), with Phoebe biting her lip and trying not to cry.

They took me to some cop-shop or other and pushed me in to just the kind of interview room I'd been expecting. Perhaps that was why I couldn't take it seriously, because it felt like I was in one of those appalling Edgar Lustgarten Scotland Yard movies which still turn up on satellite. I always thought the acting in them was crap, until Howard and Martin showed me that the actors deserved Oscars for getting it just right.

We went through it once, and then we went through it again. I must admit the second time sounded thinner, but I still couldn't believe that anything serious was going to happen.

Howard summed up the evidence against me so far – no papers, no gas mask, no friends or relations . . . Martin added that I had fair hair and blue eyes. I pointed out that he had as well, to which he blurted that his grandmother was Dutch.

One up to the Mighty Sparrow!

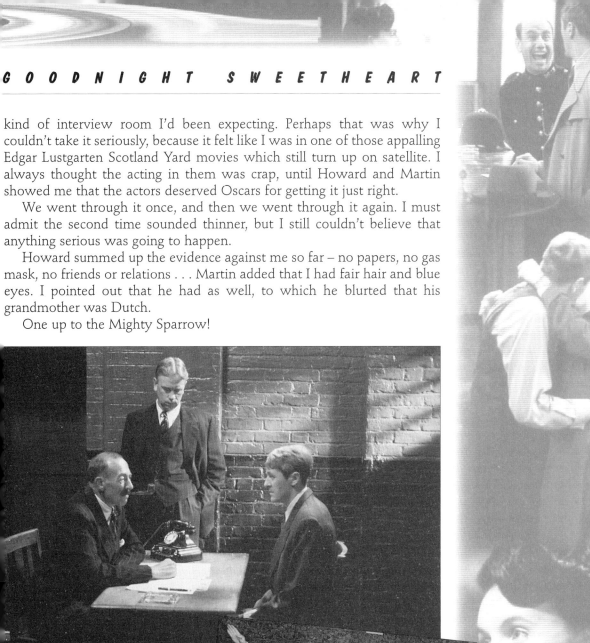

The Serious Cliché Squad giving me a hard time about Nazi hair colours

While he was thinking about it, I said that Hitler had brown hair, Goebbels had black hair, and Goering had sort of chestnut hair, though I thought he dyed it.

They wanted to know how I knew so much about Nazi hair. 'Because I was Hitler's barber of course!' I said, adding for effect: 'Something for the weekend, Adolf? Ja, Poland please Gary! But we fell out when he wouldn't let me cut his fringe . . .'

Howard, a man with no sense of humour, told me I was up to my neck in S H one T, so I got serious and explained that I'd seen them all on the newsreels.

One down to the Sparrow, since I forgot that Howard would only have seen them in black and white.

I mumbled something about America, and we went through that again, how I had spent three years there studying wireless, and was now working in top secret radio research with the Yanks . . .

Howard said the Americans weren't in the war, and I said not officially, looking suitably mysterious. When he demanded to know the name of my boss, I said I was sworn to secrecy. I thought I was getting away with it until Martin suddenly said: 'Derek Milton'.

This Milton turned out to be a former East End copper now working with intelligence, and obviously an old mate of the grisly duo. They phoned him.

Not surprisingly, good old Derek had never heard of me, which set my brain into top gear, particularly when they started making cracks about the Tower of London and a choice of final meal. Then I had a flash, a brilliant flash!

'If I wasn't genuine,' I said, 'how would I know that Mr Churchill and President Roosevelt have just concluded a secret arms deal to equip ten British divisions?' They checked with Derek, and bingo! 'I'm sorry, Mr Sparrow. Sorry to put you to any inconvenience, Sir. Here's your coat, your hat. Oh, let me brush off that speck of dust, Mr Sparrow. Any trouble in future, just ask for me by name, Sir.'

The only trouble was, it was 9 a.m., and a certain Mrs Yvonne Sparrow would be standing behind the front door with a carving knife. But what could I do? I went home to face the music, and was surprised to get a passionate hug rather than a knee in the goolies. I was also surprised to see Ron there, but there wasn't time to ask why.

I mumbled something about delivering a baby, but Yvonne cut across me. She thought I'd been caught up in the bombing. Which was the most gob-smacking thing she could have said and left me, yet again, looking bemused.

. SUNDAY 30 .

Just time for a quickie while Yvonne's gone to the garden centre to help Stella look at plants.

That bombing thing wasn't sinister at all, though it might have been, thanks to bloody Ron. I MUST TALK TO RON!

It turns out there was an IRA explosion in Holborn, which was where I was meant to be getting my circuit-tester. Phew! We celebrated with a quickie, during which Yvonne managed to ruin my concentration by saying that the bedroom was starting to look shabby! Honestly, what a thing to say in the throes of passion. I admit I was thinking of John Selwyn Gummer at the time – well, it always helps me last longer – but she didn't know that.

It turns out she hadn't slept all night, and had been phoning round everyone she knew, as well as calling the police every five minutes. Stella was on night-shift, but she'd sent Ron round to keep Yvonne company, which she found a bit of a mixed blessing. Apparently he asked for Camp coffee! A strange man indeed.

Yvonne said she thought I might be in the 1940s theme pub, and Ron came over all mysterious. Thank God her mind wasn't really on it. He went into this riff about whether the world as we know it is the be-all and end-all of physical existence, which Yvonne immediately identified as

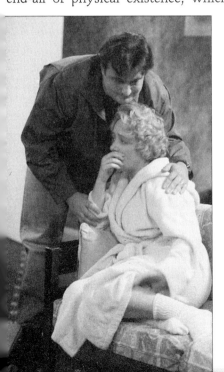

metaphysics. She's clever, my wife. Ron wasn't sure without looking the word up in a dictionary, but he did tell her that maybe I'd stumbled through a weak point in the space time continuum and found myself in a parallel universe, but at another point in history.

Yvonne told me she thinks he's barking mad, which is a great relief. She tried to get him to go home, but he'd promised Stella he'd stay, so he stayed. At least he took Yvonne's mind off her own theory that I had another woman. She laughed at the silliness of it, which was more than a bit insulting.

Ron tries to comfort an anxious
Yvonne. She doesn't always wear a
dressing gown

NOVEMBER

Sitting in the van with the pen in one hand and a sandwich in the other. It's hard writing on prawn stains.

Strange day, yesterday. I popped into Wally's World of Wallpaper on the way home and picked up loads of décor stuff – catalogues, swatches, wallpaper books, paint cards. I thought if I did something about the bedroom, then it would make Yvonne happy.

Being a serious bloke, I was taking it seriously, but it was almost as if she'd forgotten she ever mentioned the bedroom was shabby. She just made a crack about me turning into Pierre le Pouffe, décor for the decadent.

So I chided her for being homophobic and, bosh, we were into the middle of a heavy discussion about our sex life. Naturally I tried to keep it light, wondering if my foreplay technique needed a light sanding down and rag roll, but she was all for the heavy chat and serious analysis.

Why do women always want to talk about things in depth, over a period of hours, when a couple of brisk one-liners could solve the problem?

Blokes never agonize that way. 'Couldn't get it up last night?' 'Never mind, mate, there's always tomorrow. Pint?' 'Don't mind if I do.'

When I suggested there was too much emphasis on the physical side of marriage these days, it didn't go down well, nor did my little joke about when the earth moved during the war it was usually a land mine.

And all because I was going to decorate the bedroom while she was away on her Open University weekend in Huddersfield, about which I'd already made a few subtle remarks. Like those weekends being notorious drunken shagfests.

So we had a row about that instead, with Yvonne saying she'd been working on her essay for two months to impress her tutor, me saying that maybe she should pack her G-string as well, her pretending to be horrified at the suggestion that she'd screw her tutor to get a good grade, me apologizing, and her (as usual) getting the last word by saying that she'd get a good grade because it was a bloody good essay, then she'd screw her tutor because he's gorgeous.

A cosy domestic scene as we dicuss wallpaper samples. A more difficult one as I persuade Ron to print me some wartime identity papers

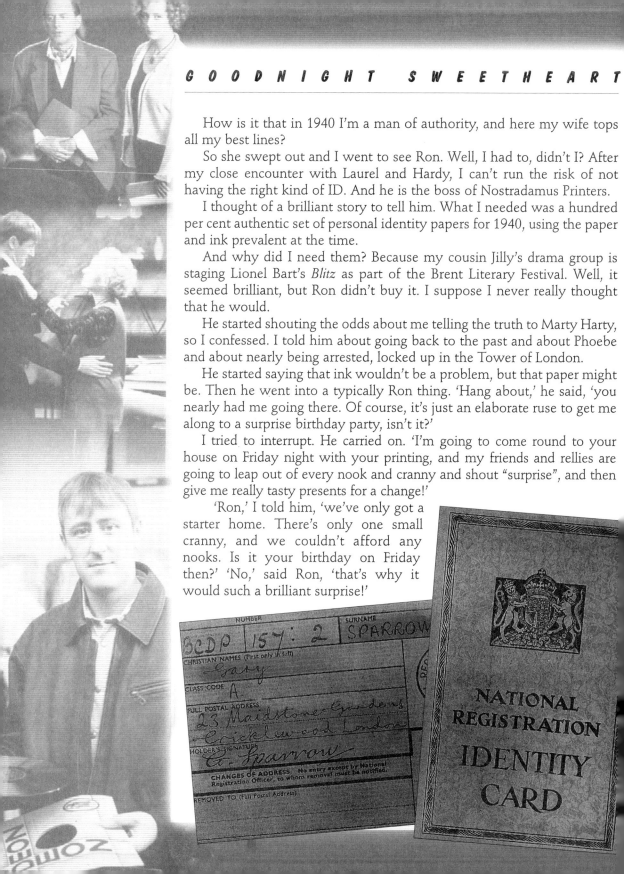

How is it that in 1940 I'm a man of authority, and here my wife tops all my best lines?

So she swept out and I went to see Ron. Well, I had to, didn't I? After my close encounter with Laurel and Hardy, I can't run the risk of not having the right kind of ID. And he is the boss of Nostradamus Printers.

I thought of a brilliant story to tell him. What I needed was a hundred per cent authentic set of personal identity papers for 1940, using the paper and ink prevalent at the time.

And why did I need them? Because my cousin Jilly's drama group is staging Lionel Bart's *Blitz* as part of the Brent Literary Festival. Well, it seemed brilliant, but Ron didn't buy it. I suppose I never really thought that he would.

He started shouting the odds about me telling the truth to Marty Harty, so I confessed. I told him about going back to the past and about Phoebe and about nearly being arrested, locked up in the Tower of London.

He started saying that ink wouldn't be a problem, but that paper might be. Then he went into a typically Ron thing. 'Hang about,' he said, 'you nearly had me going there. Of course, it's just an elaborate ruse to get me along to a surprise birthday party, isn't it?'

I tried to interrupt. He carried on. 'I'm going to come round to your house on Friday night with your printing, and my friends and rellies are going to leap out of every nook and cranny and shout "surprise", and then give me really tasty presents for a change!'

'Ron,' I told him, 'we've only got a starter home. There's only one small cranny, and we couldn't afford any nooks. Is it your birthday on Friday then?' 'No,' said Ron, 'that's why it would such a brilliant surprise!'

When all this started, I thought I was mad, but Ron really *is* mad.

He saw by my face that I was deadly serious, and calmed down. He wanted to know whether Phoebe was willing, and called her a tart, which was totally out of order. I told him: 'She's a very sweet, unspoiled young woman whose husband is serving with Monty in North Africa'.

He took that in, then got all meditative and said that even if I did sleep with her, then it wouldn't be adultery technically since I wouldn't have been born then, and she's probably been dead for years.

That made me feel uncomfortable, I don't know why. After all, I do want to sleep with Phoebe. I do want to take her in my arms and discover her body and . . .

Anyway, Ron said he'd do my documents under one condition, that I should take him back with me. I'd never thought of that.

FRIDAY 4.

Actually, it's Monday the seventh, but there's so much happening I'm going to try and write what happened under the date that it happened, if that makes sense. Well, I understand it, and nobody is going to read this but me.

Friday morning, Yvonne comes downstairs with the suitcase from the attic with all the 1940s stuff I've been hiding because I don't want her to see how much of it there is. I'm having my bran flakes and listening to Sonny Boy Williamson (*Fattening Frogs and Snakes*, to be precise), when she turns the music off, turns me round and shows me the case.

I must admit it looked rather odd; clothes, shoes, books, videos, presents for Phoebe . . . quite an impressive collection, though I say so myself.

Yvonne wondered whether I had a fantasy about secretly dressing up as Trevor Howard and hanging round railway stations trying to seduce Celia Johnson look-alikes with presents of stockings and cheap perfume.

I told her there was a perfectly rational explanation, though for the life of me I couldn't think of one. Then one struck me. Of course! It was all stuff for a surprise birthday party!

Yvonne pointed out that her birthday was in March, and that on the believability index I came slightly below the Tory Party manifesto.

So I spoke the truth. I said I wore the clothes to go back to 1940 to see my girlfriend and take her presents.

Yvonne didn't believe me. In fact, she recommended psychiatric help. Then she took the case, packed and left without another word.

I wonder if she really is going to screw her tutor? And would I really mind?

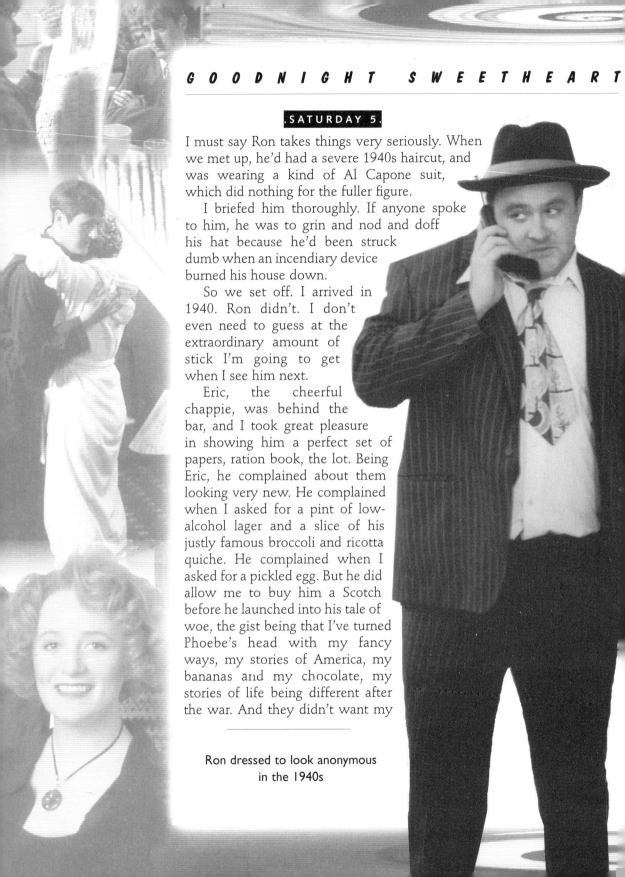

.SATURDAY 5.

I must say Ron takes things very seriously. When we met up, he'd had a severe 1940s haircut, and was wearing a kind of Al Capone suit, which did nothing for the fuller figure.

I briefed him thoroughly. If anyone spoke to him, he was to grin and nod and doff his hat because he'd been struck dumb when an incendiary device burned his house down.

So we set off. I arrived in 1940. Ron didn't. I don't even need to guess at the extraordinary amount of stick I'm going to get when I see him next.

Eric, the cheerful chappie, was behind the bar, and I took great pleasure in showing him a perfect set of papers, ration book, the lot. Being Eric, he complained about them looking very new. He complained when I asked for a pint of low-alcohol lager and a slice of his justly famous broccoli and ricotta quiche. He complained when I asked for a pickled egg. But he did allow me to buy him a Scotch before he launched into his tale of woe, the gist being that I've turned Phoebe's head with my fancy ways, my stories of America, my bananas and my chocolate, my stories of life being different after the war. And they didn't want my

Ron dressed to look anonymous in the 1940s

handouts, thank you very much. When I said I'd brought Phoebe some cigarettes, he said he'd be happy to take them off my hands.

Then he made my heart turn over by telling me that Phoebe had left home. Given his diatribe, I naturally assumed it was because of me, but Eric told me not to be conceited, perhaps the first sensible thing I've heard him say. Apparently she decided she wanted to get a job or do something useful for the war effort, so she went to stay with her aunt. Naturally Eric refused to give me the address, though he changed his tune when I offered him a bar of chocolate.

He'd just told me where she was living when Phoebe herself appeared, looking really pale and very distressed. I went to put my arm around her, so did Eric. He tried to push my arm away, and we jostled over the unfortunate Phoebe until she told her father to stop.

She'd been to the market – someone said they'd seen some oranges – and when she got back she found that her aunt's house had been bombed. Her aunt was in hospital with a broken leg, the house was gone, along with half her clothes. She cried a little.

Eric told her she should move back with him, but Phoebe said she wasn't sure she wanted to. She was a grown woman. Eric rounded on me, and we had another silly argument. Phoebe stopped it by walking out. He is such a stupid old bugger!

I ran after Phoebe, and caught her up at the gates of a graveyard, probably not the best place for a walk under the circumstances. She linked her arm through mine, and we didn't talk for a while. Suddenly she burst out with the news that the house next door had taken a direct hit, two dead, one missing . . . the husband would come home from work to find no family and a big hole in the ground where his house used to be.

'It could have been me,' Phoebe said, then burst out, 'I hate this bloody war.'

I'd never heard her swear before.

'I haven't nearly been killed before,' she said. 'Don't you hate it, Gary?'

Phoebe in a state of shock after a bomb hit the house next door

I said I did.

'Do you?', she asked. 'Because it don't seem to affect you like it does other people. You come and go, you're always happy, shortages and rationing don't seem to bother you. Why? How do you manage it?'

I said that, deep down inside, I knew we were going to win.

Sometimes it's dreadful to have so much information, to know what's going to happen, how many people are going to be killed, how much pain and misery there's going to be for Phoebe and Reg and even bloody Eric. I can tell her things will be all right, but why should she believe me? There she is, desperate for an orange, when I can bring her a whole crate of oranges without thinking.

Then an awful thing happened. Phoebe asked me to take her back with me. I was totally thrown, because I thought she meant back to the present. But of course she meant back to Cricklewood in 1940, not 1994.

She looked absolutely desperate. Surely I had some family or a mate or knew someone with a spare room? God help me, I tried to stall her by saying that Cricklewood got bombed too. I even tried a joke, telling her the glue factory had taken a terrible pasting. She didn't get it. She thought what was bothering me was that I didn't want people to think I was taking advantage of a married woman. I said I'd like to take advantage, but I didn't want people to think I was. At least she laughed. But it didn't last; she got all serious again.

Donald had written, but the letter said nothing, or at least nothing intimate, just stuff about the weather and how he hoped she was keeping well. I tried to suggest that some people weren't good letter-writers. Phoebe wasn't having any of it. She was sure that Donald had nothing to say because he doesn't really care about her. Then she quoted back at me stuff I'd said about people not being forced to stay in loveless marriages after the war, and did I mean it? She looked at me like she looked at me in the tube station, hopeful, vulnerable. I felt like a bastard.

I'm so confused! I want Phoebe more than anything else in the world, but I feel so guilty about Yvonne. If only she was stroppy all the time, then I'd really go for it with Phoebe. But Yvonne's under a lot of pressure and even though she bullies me she does it because she loves me. I had a sudden flash of Yvonne and her tutor, and it made me really jealous.

Fortunately it started to rain, so we made a dash for a little chapel. Phoebe looked up at the cross on the altar and said, 'I bet God knows'. I thought she meant us, but she meant whether we were going to win the war. When we sat down, Phoebe got a splinter in her leg from the pew, which didn't help, but I gave her some of the stuff I'd been collecting – stockings, Hershey Bars, cigarettes . . .

I thought that asking about her wanting a job would be a neutral thing to talk about, and she said that before the war she used to work in a shoe shop next door to the People's Palace. Once she sold a pair of spats to Joe Loss. I was suitably impressed. She said Joe was very smart, very dapper, but when the war started they needed leather to make army boots, so she was out of work. Now she was thinking about doing something for the war effort, but Eric was scared of her becoming independent. I wasn't scared of that, was I?

I told her that most of the troubles in my marriage started when Marilyn got a job she thought was more important than mine. Phoebe looked horrified. I'd forgotten that I'd talked about Marilyn as someone I went out with, not as a wife. So I improvised. Again. 'Well,' I said, 'she got involved in drink and drugs, and got mixed up with a pair of over-sexed brothers called the Kennedys . . . '

Phoebe didn't seem too worried about Marilyn, since she was still looking for a home. 'Where do you live?' she wanted to know. 'Just a little house,' I said, 'only two bedrooms.' Wrong answer. A crappy starter-home in Cricklewood sounded like a palace to Phoebe, who immediately wanted to move into the spare room. I tried the line about not wanting people to think I was taking advantage, which didn't work. I mentioned Eric. Phoebe said he could think what he wanted.

What could I do? I lied that I had lied when I said Marilyn was in America. In fact, she was here in England, in Cricklewood, living with me.

Phoebe went ape-shit, calling me a two-timing creep. I said I'd pay for her to rent a flat, but that made things worse. She thought I was suggesting a sort of mistress arrangement. When she stormed off, I thought it was more sensible not to follow.

But I felt about so big when I got home, and really empty inside. There was the woman I love, well, one of the women I love, asking me for help to get her away from danger. There was me piling lie on top of lie, sending her back into the Blitz. Not good at all.

I was thinking about what to do when I saw the answering machine light flashing, and pressed the button to hear an outraged message from Ron, who thinks I've made a mug of him. He was threatening to drive up to Huddersfield and tell Yvonne all about it. There was only one thing to do. Drive to Huddersfield myself. So I did.

I got there about nine. A security guard pointed me towards the Harold Wilson coffee bar where, he said, the OU course was having its pre-orgy barbecue, ho ho. I'd just set off in that direction when there was a loud explosion. Naturally I threw myself to the ground, shouting at the security guard to get down. He seemed bemused at my reaction to fireworks. I stood up again, brushed myself down, and made my way to the coffee bar with as much dignity as I could muster.

The scene inside was just as I thought – low lights, soft music, and Yvonne smooching with a fifty-year-old creep who had leather elbow patches on his sports jacket. I went over, tapped the creep on the shoulder,

Yvonne, with Hillary Clinton hair for the occasion, gets to grips with a leather-patch man at her OU weekend. She's a lot happier with me

then walked away. Yvonne came running after me. When she said she hadn't seen Ron, I relaxed and played the jealousy card. It went down a treat. Yvonne assured me there wasn't anyone else, and invited me up to her room for 'a bottle of Rioja and a bit of a seeing-to'.

On the way out, I just froze. I heard Phoebe in my head saying: 'Take me back, Gary'. I heard myself talking about Marilyn. From being jealous of Yvonne, I now felt I was betraying Phoebe.

So I pulled Yvonne on to the dance floor, and taught her to fox trot to Chris Montez.

.SUNDAY 6.

Spent much of the night thinking of John Selwyn Gummer. Then I drove 200 miles back home, read the papers, couldn't concentrate, and thought about what to do. It seems to me there's only one thing to do – forget about Phoebe, forget about time-travelling, walk the other way if I see the present PC Deadman, and concentrate on my marriage. Yvonne can be quite inventive when she puts her mind to it, and she was so pleased to see me in Huddersfield. As for Phoebe, what can I do? I can't give her what she wants or what she needs, apart from stockings and soft fruit. All that take-me-back stuff proves it. So no more 1940. I certainly won't miss Eric.

On the other hand, the Ron problem needs to be solved. I donned my suit for the last time, made a quick trip into the past, bought a paper and came back. I must say the wartime *Daily Mirror* was a bit tame.

After I'd flicked through that, and the *Sport* (surely Busty Bernice's Twin Bazookas can't be natural?), I got bored. So I went up to the attic, brought down my electronic keyboard, and gave 'Superstition' a good going over. I'd forgotten how good those keyboards are. Set it up right, and you can sound like a jazz funk band with just one finger.

The doorbell rang. It was a stroppy young charity collector. I offered her my original 1940s suit, a museum piece really, but she turned up her nose at it, and was marching off just as Yvonne came home, full of herself. Her dissertation got a terrific reaction apparently – Fantasy, Reality and Obsession: A Case Study, would you believe. Naturally, I asked if it was about me. Well, you can't be too careful. I was still holding my suit, and I explained about the charity collector. Yvonne seemed a bit miffed that her surprise party was off, but she was all enthusiastic about having got through the heavy stage of her course and being able to relax more and devote more time to me and my interests, whatever they might be at the moment.

Then she suggested dancing classes, thanks to our foxtrot. Oh well, anything for a quiet life.

.MONDAY 7.

Went to see Ron first thing, just as he was opening his shutters. He was not a happy person. As far as he's concerned, I'm a 'sick practical joker, a second-rate Jeremy Beadle' . . . He was convinced I'd hidden somewhere in Duckett's Passage, rather than really going back. He had enough hump

Convincing Ron can be hard work,
but I usually manage it

for the Camel Corps, and Stella hated his haircut. When it was longer, she used to hang on to it in moments of passion. Now it's no hair, no passion. Oh dear.

Anyway, I apologized, thanked him for not grassing me up to Yvonne, and then I gave him the 1940 *Daily Mirror*. He looked at it closely. He felt the paper. He looked at his hands. They had ink on them. He was convinced. But why, he wanted to know, couldn't he go back? Was it just because he didn't believe?

I hated to let him down, but I don't think it's anything to do with belief or non-belief . . . After all, the first time I went back, I didn't even know there was a back to go to. And anyway, after my unhappy experience with Phoebe, I wouldn't be going back any more.

He suggested a drink, but I said I was learning ballroom dancing. Ron looked bemused.

At lunchtime I went to a suit shop and hired a little surprise for Yvonne. So, just as she finished pushing back the furniture and was poised to put the teaching video in the machine, I made my grand entrance in white tie and tails. She laughed a lot, and wondered why I went into everything with a 150 per cent over-the-top attitude. I said it had to be because I

Fred and Ginger Sparrow,
tripping the light fantastic

wasn't breast fed long enough, or too long, or too much from one side. Then she made a very mysterious remark, about what I had said explaining something. Wonder what she meant?

So she started the video and we tripped the light fantastic. Well, we both tripped a lot, but it didn't seem too hard to get the hang of. After a while, she suggested changing the video – for something to do with 'martial arts', which was a bit of a surprise. Yvonne said it was 'marital arts' and went upstairs to slip into something Anne Summersy.

I ejected the dance video and was about to shove in the marital arts when I caught the end of the local news. It was a story about a plucky old-age pensioner seeing off two hooligans with her husband's World War II revolver. Her name was Phoebe Sparrow from Bethnal Green.

When Yvonne came back in her flimsy little number she found me staring blankly at the screen. Of course, I couldn't say why. I also found it difficult to raise a flicker of interest in marital arts, the end result being one of those frosty nights and a strong recommendation for counselling.

.TUESDAY 8.

I went to see Ron again. Good old Ron, I'd be lost without him. I wanted some advice. Phoebe Sparrow – we must have got married. Ron thought that wasn't necessarily true. She might have married another Sparrow. Or just adopted my name in a wistful attempt to keep alight the last embers of our brief unfulfilled relationship (he's a poet).

'But,' I said, 'if we did get married and I never returned to the past, then I'd be changing the course of history.' Ron thought I stood that risk every time I went back, but I told him my Grandpa Gareth, the submariner, would have been around then, name on the electoral roll, etc.

Ron told me to go and see the battling granny, but I thought the shock could kill her, and in any case Phoebe believed I was already married – to Marilyn Monroe. That really cracked him up, particularly since he'd been printing some cards of Marilyn. He gave me one, suitably inscribed.

No, I had to go back and brave seeing Phoebe, but I needed an alibi for Yvonne.

The back page of the paper on Ron's desk gave me an inspiration. England were playing Lithuania away the following night. If I told Yvonne that Ron and I had been offered a couple of tickets . . .

Ron said he'd cover for me, but I insisted that he actually went. Doing a quick calculation, I reckoned I had enough in the building society to pay for him. Ron didn't seem to mind.

The return of the hooligan

.WEDNESDAY 9.

I wore my England shirt at breakfast to make it look good. Actually, it was an old England shirt, since I don't have the finance to subsidize Umbro. Yvonne couldn't believe that I was going, since, after my last live experience of England, I'd looked in the Yellow Pages for a

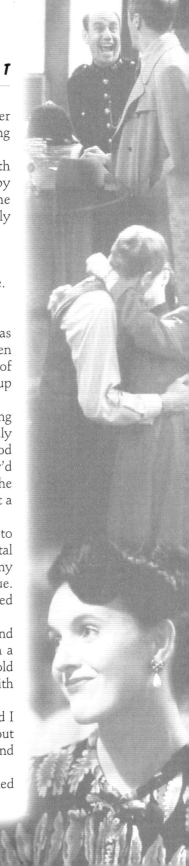

hitman to assassinate Graham Taylor. I explained that hating the manager and despising his team selection was the only pleasure of supporting England. If only I'd known who to bung when Taylor went.

She gave me a dodgy moment when she suggested coming with me, before admitting it was only a wind-up. Then she amazed me by telling me to buy condoms at the airport, but that was only because she wanted me to swop them for caviar – condoms being in short supply in Vilnius.

THURSDAY 10.

Went to 1940, found a pea-souper, got knocked down. By an ambulance.

FRIDAY 11.

Came to and heard Phoebe talking to Reg. Felt like a dream. Phoebe was saying she hoped I'd died in my sleep, without suffering. Reg said I'd been drugged up with morphine, catapulted into their lives in a moment of crisis, yet always out of step with the time. I thought it was time to sit up and declare I was still alive.

Reg assured me that I was, and Phoebe explained they'd been talking about Mr Chamberlain, who had just snuffed it. As for me, I had a badly sprained wrist, mild concussion, bruising and contusions. But it was good riddance to Chamberlain and appeasers like him and Baldwin. If they'd stopped Hitler in 1936 when he re-militarized the Rhineland . . . She stopped when she saw my amazed look, and assured me she wasn't just a pretty face. I squeezed her hand.

Reg said I'd been talking a lot in my sleep, taking out his notebook to refresh his memory. Apparently I'd said Hi-8 camcorder, Nicam digital stereo, something about laser discs. What on earth was going on in my mind? When I'm unconscious, I must think like a Dixon's catalogue. Naturally, I told Reg to forget it because it was all top secret. He nodded seriously, then ate the page from his notebook. I like Reg.

But it felt like time to go. When I stood up, I nearly fell over. Phoebe and Reg helped me back to bed, Phoebe tut-tutting that I seemed to be in a hurry to get back to Marilyn. Reg showed some interest, so Phoebe told him Marilyn was my wife and then sent him away for a cup of tea with his mate in the mortuary so that we could talk.

I was amazed that Phoebe was there after our last conversation, and I told her so. She said she'd been a bit hasty. After all, when I talked about people not living in loveless marriages after the war, it wasn't just her and Donald I was describing, but me and Marilyn too.

Then she said something amazing, that she thought we were destined

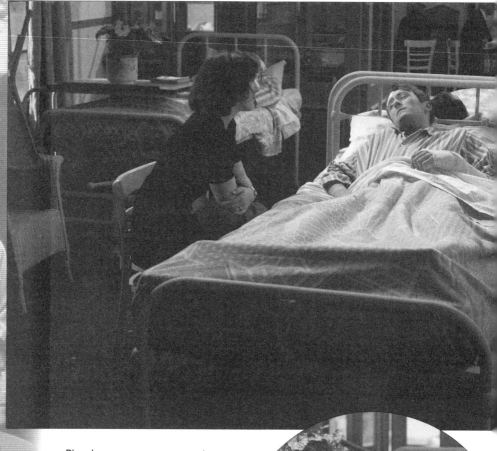

Phoebe comes to see me in hospital – she's a princess

to be together, that there was a purpose to life, and it wasn't just a big game of chance. We looked at one another. Once again I wanted to be nowhere else but with Phoebe.

This time it was Reg who got in the way of a tender moment. Why does someone always interrupt our tender moments?

He'd brought my belongings in a brown paper bag, along with my suit. I reached for the bag, but he insisted on itemizing everything in his annoying, copper-like way. He did the suit, the blood-stained shirt, the underpants. I got rather tetchy, but it didn't put him off at all. He did the broken watch, the wallet, and the contents of the wallet, including a picture of a rather glamorous blonde signed – All my love, Marilyn. Ron's postcard!

I tried to grab the picture, but I couldn't reach, and Phoebe asked to see it. Reg was letching over it, and wouldn't let go. He seemed sad that Mrs Deadman would never have her picture taken bursting out of her dress. Then he showed it to Phoebe before looking at the address on my ration book – grandpa Gareth's address in fact. Reg seemed very keen to pop round and assure Marilyn of my safety, even though I told him not to bother. He wondered whether the grating was anywhere near my house and went away, still clutching the picture.

Phoebe looked very depressed. She said she must be bonkers to think I'd prefer her to a glamorous blonde like MM. Another tender moment loomed, another sodding interruption! This time it was Eric, who shooed Phoebe back to the pub and plonked himself down on my bed.

As usual, he was in a strop, calling me a two-timing gigolo and accusing me of staging the accident to win my way back into Phoebe's affections. Silly old fool. He had a complicated theory about me trying to get in with Phoebe, turn her off Donald, and walk into the tenancy of the Royal Oak when he snuffed it. He was still ranting on when I felt faint and nearly passed out. Luckily a nurse saw me, chucked Eric out and called for a doctor. Which meant I was in for another night. Well, it gave me time to work out a story for Yvonne.

SATURDAY 12.

When I woke up, I felt better, a lot better. But I didn't want to go back without seeing Phoebe, and I was sure she'd visit. I'd just finished dressing when she walked in, surprised to see me up and about, but definitely glum. She'd obviously been brooding about her and me and Marilyn, and talked herself into thinking she didn't have a chance. Oh Phoebe, if only you knew!

I blurted out that I'd be hell to live with, always coming and going unannounced, spending weeks away, never able to tell her what I was up to. She didn't quite get it, and I was going to explain more when there was a double interruption – Eric turned up with Deadman. Sometimes I feel my life is like a sitcom.

Eric started ranting about how he had forbidden Phoebe ever to see me again, me a married man with a wife in Cricklewood. Reg interrupted him, and spoke kindly to me. He didn't quite know how to put it, but he had been over to see my wife (who didn't look very like her picture in a head scarf and a pinny), and that a hulking great chap in a submariner's pullover had appeared in the doorway. So it looked as if my Marilyn had 'a bit on the side'.

I apologized to grandfather Gareth in my head. Given Reg's unique way with words, he must be a very confused man at this moment.

Eric chipped in that she obviously had taste, getting involved with a real fighting man rather than a pansy like me. Phoebe insisted I wasn't a pansy, and said I would be going straight round to sort the bloke out.

What could I do? People were looking. I pleaded for privacy to recover from the shock and they left. But Phoebe, wonderful Phoebe, came back, full of sympathy and wondering when she'd see me again. I had to be truthful. I said I didn't know when I would see her, or what we could do. We were just about to kiss when Eric shouted for her and she left. I gave them time to get clear, then I left too.

I can't say I was looking forward to seeing Yvonne, without any idea of what Ron might have told her.

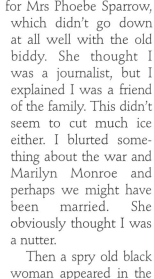

I hung around on the doorstep for a minute or two feeling nervous. Then I turned the key in the lock and went in, bruised and bandaged, to face the music.

Yvonne surprised me immediately by saying that the Lithuanian police had obviously given me a good hiding. What??? She said Ron had told her everything, and how could I have exposed myself in the streets of Vilnius, especially in November. I'll swing for that bloke! Then, with a dig about me trying to mature into an adult while she was away, she swept off to see sister Alison. I went straight for the phone book, looked up Sparrow, and got back in my van to visit the battling granny. I just had to know.

For the second time in an hour I stood on a doorstep wondering what to say and what I was going to find. But I had to find out. I rang the bell. After a bit, an old woman came to the door. Was she Phoebe? Had she been Phoebe? It was hard to tell. I said I was looking for Mrs Phoebe Sparrow, which didn't go down at all well with the old biddy. She thought I was a journalist, but I explained I was a friend of the family. This didn't seem to cut much ice either. I blurted something about the war and Marilyn Monroe and perhaps we might have been married. She obviously thought I was a nutter.

Then a spry old black woman appeared in the hall, wanting to know what the matter was. The first woman called her Phoebe. Relief just doesn't do justice to my smile.

Twenty-eight incendiaries hit St Paul's Cathedral. Miraculously, the building survived

.SUNDAY 13.

Went for a pint with Ron to find out what he'd been saying to Yvonne. She saw me off with a crack about it being nice out, but to make sure I kept it zipped away. Apparently he'd popped round in all innocence to find out how I'd got on, discovered I wasn't there, tried to cover for me, but fell apart when Yvonne threatened him with the nutcrackers. So he'd concocted this Ron story about mistaking a museum for a pub, and a regrettable incident involving a Zippo lighter, a bottle of damson brandy, and a 700-year-old tapestry.

The curator had called the cops, and the last he'd seen of me was running round the red-light district of Vilnius, wearing nothing but a Union Jack and pursued by the riot police. He seemed to feel that the story deserved a pint. I told him it deserved a thick lip. Pillock!

.MONDAY 14.

Decided definitely not to see Phoebe again. It's not fair to keep raising her hopes, then dashing them. What a strange phrase. I wonder why hopes are dashed? But that's it, the end, finito.

Things frostier than Vilnius at home.

.WEDNESDAY 16.

Still frosty. Found myself in the East End with a bit of time, felt like a quick half to cheer myself up . . .

Phoebe was really pleased to see me, and Reg had some top secret news, which he insisted on sharing. Apparently, the King is coming to visit the London Hospital. Phoebe got very excited and said she'd kill to see him.

She and her friend Beryl slept on Horse Guards to be sure of seeing his Coronation procession.

I made the mistake of voicing some mildly republican sentiments, i.e., that the King is just a human being, tossing in the fact that fifty years from now – I mean then – Japanese tourists will be having guided tours of Buckingham Palace.

Eric didn't like that at all. When Reg refused to arrest me for treason, Eric barred me. For life. Just as well, really. It means Phoebe can blame her dad for breaking us up.

Bought some flowers and got home to find Yvonne ironing her things but not mine. Felt like permafrost. With what can only be described as a flourish, she whipped out our Access bill and thrust it at me. I hadn't realized quite how much I'd been spending on the World War II stuff. Then she gave me page 2.

I mumbled a bit about cutting back, and offered to do the dinner.

There's isn't any, Yvonne said. I wondered why not. She told me why not . . . 'I spent an hour going round the supermarket,' Yvonne said, 'got to the check-out, presented my credit card, and saw the machine reject it in front of a long queue of people, one of whom was Linda Ferguson from over the road, who's always thought she's a cut above us because they've got an integral garage. How do you think I felt?'

'Embarrassed?', I suggested. She added: 'Humiliated, angry and upset.' I said: 'It wasn't Linda Ferguson's fault.' 'No,' said Yvonne, 'it's your fault, Gary. It's not much fun being the only woman in England still suffering from the Blitz. If I didn't know you better, I'd think you were having an affair.' Then she added: 'Gary, I'm carrying this marriage, I'm carrying you, and I'm fed up! Ever since you started this 1940s fixation, it's like you're not really here. So get rid of it, or get rid me of me!'

It seemed a bit unreasonable really, but in another way she has a point. That bit about me not really being there since I started my 1940s thing hit home. So I went to see Ron to ask if he'd take the stuff off my hands. He said he didn't want his own Imperial War Museum, but he'd happily store the stuff for me if I wanted to go on seeing Phoebe, which I didn't. Well, I'm sure I don't really.

The trouble is, part of me wants to stay in the past, and I told Ron that. He said he knew just how I felt – I was besotted with Phoebe, she haunted my every waking moment as she haunted my dreams. And she does. Then he spoiled it by saying he'd felt just the same way about Cilla Black when he was nine, before trying to convince me that men aren't naturally monogamous and I shouldn't dump Phoebe.

I should have realized he had something in mind. The result is that I now possess £250 in perfectly printed period fivers, to invest in Arbuthnot Brothers of Ealing, which turned into Eurotronics Plc. Well, even I've heard of the said multi-national media giant.

The fact that I want to say a proper goodbye to Phoebe, as well as the possibility of becoming a millionaire, means I'm going back. Though I do worry a lot about meddling in history.

What if I've been given the gift of time-travel for a reason I don't know about yet? Perhaps, somehow, I change the course of the war but never make the history books. I'm confused.

THURSDAY 17

Think I'll leave going back for a bit. Let Eric cool down. Work out how to get Ron's shares. I don't suppose many stockbrokers drink in the Royal Oak. Maybe that ARP bloke could help? He owes me one for turning me in.

WRITTEN LATER BUT STILL TODAY

Yvonne still giving me gyp about getting rid of the gear, so I've started packing it up. I suppose there is quite a lot when you think about it.

I put an old newsreel in for a last look, and I was stunned! Talk about altering the course of history! The commentator bloke (where did they find them?) was chuntering on in the usual clipped way when he said something about the King and Queen visiting The London Hospital on Tuesday and lunch being delayed a bit. So I glanced at the screen. And it was me. And Phoebe, and Eric and Reg. Unless we all have doubles, which I doubt.

So I do see Phoebe again. Wonder if I turn up on any other newsreel?

I heard Yvonne coming, switched off the video, and got back to the packing. She thawed a bit when she saw what I was doing. She sounded almost kind.

I said there was a 1940s memorabilia fair in Runcorn at the weekend. I could stay with Ron's brother, shift the lot, and maybe even make a few quid. Yvonne seemed almost sorry for making me get rid of the stuff. Women, eh?

FRIDAY 18

Who wants to be a millionaire? What a stupid question.

.SATURDAY 19.

Bounced confidently into the Royal Oak, to be met by Eric's smiling face. Naturally I'm lying. He kept trying to chuck me out while I was telling him that the King and Queen would be visiting that very afternoon. Phoebe and Reg calmed him down, and Phoebe was all agog to see them, while Reg was miffed that no one had informed him officially. Eric, rather brutally I thought, told Reg he was a bonehead.

I cheered him up by saying I had a plan, and he had a vital part to play. If he could get us some white coats from his chum at the hospital, then we could all pretend to be doctors and smuggle ourselves in. Brilliant, though I say so myself.

Everyone else thought so too. Eric went to change his collar, Phoebe went to change her dress, and even Manny from the ARP looked sad that he was going to be on duty. I noticed he was reading the financial section of the *Manchester Guardian*, which made it easier to bring up Arbuthnot Brothers.

How a miserable sod like Eric could have a lovely daughter like Phoebe is beyond me. She must take after her mum

When I told him I'd noticed what he was reading, he looked defensive and said it didn't mean he was rich. I said I just wanted some investment advice, which made him fly off the handle and give me a speech about how just because he happened to be Jewish – but a man could dream.

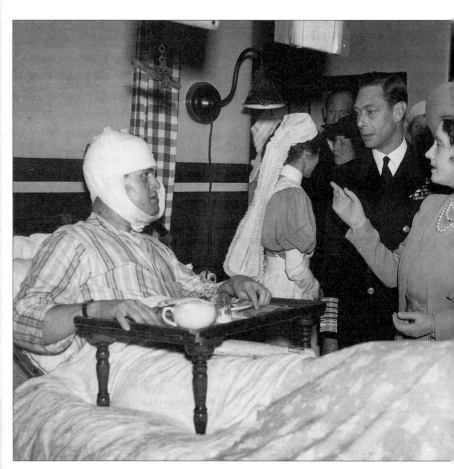

Their Majesties visit the London Hospital in 1940 ... and I was there!

'I've come into a small inheritance,' I said, 'only a few quid. But I was thinking maybe I should buy some shares.' So, Manny asked: 'What company's taken your fancy?' 'Arbuthnot Brothers Radio Limited,' I said with authority. Manny looked sceptical. 'I've got a feeling that home entertainment's going to be very big after the war,' I said. Manny looked at me pityingly.

In the end, although he obviously felt that Marks and Spencer was a better buy, he agreed to talk to his brother-in-law who dabbled a bit in the market.

Eric appeared in his new collar, and called me 'mate'. What a creep.

So off we went. Reg was waiting for us in the Commercial Road with some coats which more or less fitted, and there was a small crowd with Union Jacks, despite the secrecy. We got a few funny looks, but Reg was in full uniform, and everyone's attention was distracted by the arrival of the royal party.

I pushed Reg in front of us, made him ask a flustered-looking nurse which ward their Majesties were visiting, got directions, and headed off there. Everything and everyone looked scrubbed to within an inch of their lives, the doctors and nurses all in a line. I shoved in at the end, which didn't please the doctor I was standing beside, but I stuck out my hand and introduced myself as Dr Gareth Sparrow, Department of Experimental Plastic Surgery, and my team. He was trying to say he'd never heard of me or my team when the doors swung open, and the King and Queen were on us. It's funny to think that I've met the Queen Mum; wonder if she might remember me?

I was presenting Phoebe to the King when she crumpled at his feet in a faint. He looked quite put out. What could I say but that junior doctors worked such long hours?

The whole place went into an uproar. The King helped Phoebe up. The Queen brushed her down and asked if she was all right. Reg dropped his helmet in the excitement, tripping up a lady in waiting.

There was a lot of kerfuffle, but we got away with it, and everyone was in high spirits when we got back to the Royal Oak.

Phoebe said she was still shivering all over and her stomach was full of butterflies. Eric offered a tin of pilchards. I said the occasion demanded more than a can of dwarf Portuguese fish – it called for a slap-up meal in the West End.

Reg got all excited, and said he'd pop home for his dinner suit. I explained that I meant a meal for two, which puzzled Reg. 'What about

the others?' he asked. '*Me and Phoebe,*' I said, and could I borrow his dinner suit? He went off to fetch it with a good grace.

Mr Sparrow and Mrs Bamford dine at the Savoy. Their usual table, naturally

Eric had to put in his two penn'orth, accusing me of trying to turn Phoebe's head so that I could have my evil way with her. Trying not to blush, I said I was amazed that he could think Phoebe would betray her marriage vows for an introduction to the King, and dinner and dancing at the Savoy . . .

Phoebe gasped at the mention of the Savoy. Eric wouldn't let the subject drop, so I said I had some news that I'd wanted to break more gently. I was going away, away to Hollywood. A film company liked my composition 'On the Street Where You Live', and on the strength of it they wanted me to write a musical version of George Bernard Shaw's *Pygmalion*. Eric thought that would never be a hit.

Manny came in to find out about the visit and to say he'd introduce me to his brother-in-law, but I was more concerned with an argument Phoebe was having with Eric behind the bar. From what I could hear, she was telling Eric that Donald would never have thought of a way for her to meet the King, that I was clever, I was different, and we were in the same boat when it came to failed marriages.

Eric put in a word for Donald, but Phoebe wouldn't have it. Then he played his ace, pointing out that Donald would come back to support her and be there long after I had moved on. Phoebe trumped him. She wanted to be with me tonight, because it could be the last time. I turned away so that Manny wouldn't see the tears in my eyes.

Wearing a d-j on the tube in wartime didn't get as many funny looks as it would nowadays. I wasn't the only one in formal gear.

Phoebe was really excited and talked nineteen to the dozen. She told me how in September there'd been a demo at the Savoy, when a hundred people waited out-side until an air-raid warning, then they marched on the hotel and demanded to be let in. Apparently the un-flappable porter, or guy at the desk or whoever, waved them in, though they must have been pleased when the all-clear went after quarter of an hour.

Diner

Caviar – – 8–
Huîtres – (½-doz.) 6.–
    Les Hors d'Œuvre Variés

Saumon Fumé – 3/6
Potted Saumon – 3/–
    – 3/6

Potages.
Le Consommé Julienne aux
    Cheveux d'Ange 2/–
Le Consommé Rafraîchi – 2/–
¶ La Mousse de Sole Patience 3/6

La Crème Niçoise au Tapioca – 2/–
La Crème froide du Parisien – 2/–
Buisson de Blanchailles – 3/–

LES PLATS DU JOUR

Hot
★ Les Filets de Sole du Ténor – – 6/–
    Fillets of Sole on Leaf Spinach, Mornay Sauce with Mushrooms.
★ Le Turbot poché, Sce. Hollandaise – 5/–
    Poached Turbot. Hollandaise Sauce.
★ La Dinde poêlée Sullivan aux Céleris
    Stuffed Turkey. White Wine Sauce. Celery.   Voilés Savoy 8/–
★ Le Vol-au-Vent de Poulet des Soprano – 5/–
    Puff Paste Patties filled with Chicken, Quenelles, Mushrooms,
    Supreme Sauce, Tomatoes and Asparagus Tips.
★ Le Jambon Sous la Cendre,
    Velouté de Chicon, Sce. Porto 5/6
    Ham cooked in Paste. Madeira Sauce. Purée of Cos Lettuce.

Cold
★ Le Saumon du Tay rafraîchi
    Cold Salmon. à l'Ecossaise, Sce. Verte 6/–
★ La Mousse Yorkaise à la Gelée de Sherry
    Petite Salade Evesham 5/–
    Mousse of Ham.
★ La Fricassée de Volaille Maison – 8/–
    Cold Fricassée of Chicken.

Salade de Chicon – – 2/–
    Salade de Saison – – 2/–

Légumes.
etits Pois au Beurre – 2/6
aricots Verts – 2/6
sperges – 6/–

Pommes Mireille – 1/6
Pomme Croquette – 1/6

Entremets
Parfait Moka – 3/–
Gâteau Savoy – 3/–
    Coupe aux Fraises – 3/–

She said Eric was convinced that the nobs had an arrangement with Hitler for the West End to be left alone while the East End got a hammering. I wanted to tell her that the West End would have its share, but I just grunted.

When we got to the Savoy, the restaurant was fully booked, but I elevated my accent and pressed one of Ron's fivers on to the head waiter, which magically produced a table. Phoebe looked wonderful in her best cocktail dress, and Reg's suit fitted me quite well. I thought we made a wonderful couple, and I felt sad, despite the low chatter of up-market conversation and the not unlethal Champagne cocktails.

Phoebe stared around like a child at a Christmas party, though she was sad too. She was convinced that I'd end up with Mae West or Betty Grable, and never want to see her again. She thought Mae or Betty wouldn't be backward about coming forward in the bedroom department . . . I said I'd ask the manager if we could have a look at one, purely out of curiosity. She giggled.

I hadn't heard a thing, but apparently an air-raid siren went off, because the head waiter made a reassuring speech about the restaurant being seventy feet below ground level and there being no need to panic.

Phoebe said she didn't fancy going home in a raid, which gave me an idea. The head waiter smiled when he saw me coming; a fiver meant a lot in 1940. When I said my wife was worried about the journey back to Kensington in a raid, and did they have a room for the night, it took only another fiver to learn that the Imperial Suite was probably free.

While he was checking, I wondered whether he could organize some night-attire, toothbrushes . . . ' Certainly, Sir. My friend is the manager of Andrews and Errington in Jermyn Street, who always keep a few items of lingerie in stock for our more important patrons . . . '

As a good Liberal Democrat, I naturally deplore the privilege and servility that money buys. But it's not half enjoyable when you can flash some cash about!

I grabbed a card from a nearby salver (so much posher than a tray), scribbled on it, asked the waiter to pop it in with the nightie, and went back to Phoebe. She was worried that my soup was getting cold. I told her I'd been asking the head waiter if they had a suite. She said I was getting ahead of myself, and she might not have room for a sweet after her duck.

While I was telling her the story of my movie, trying hard to remember the interesting bits of *My Fair Lady*, strange things were happening in the present. This is Ron's account, so it may not be totally reliable, but apparently Yvonne came round to his office to say that she was worried

about me. Perhaps she was being too demanding. Women needed different things from marriage than men. And men never really seemed to understand what women wanted. Ron seemed a confident bloke with women, so what did he think she wanted, what did he think she needed?

Ron, never a man to treat things simply, immediately thought Yvonne was coming on to him, the pillock! He launched into a speech about a sensual adventure being momentarily satisfying but ultimately sterile, and was only momentarily discommoded (God, his style is catching!) when Yvonne said: 'I'd rather go to bed with Sid Vicious'. Who, as we all know, is dead.

Then she stormed off, leaving Ron to drool over a car mag and dream of the millions that I wasn't going to be organizing. But he didn't know that. I feel bad about Ron.

As it happened, Phoebe did have time for a sweet, and we were both too pissed to care about being in company when I sang her 'I Could Have Danced All Night'. A discreet cough from the head waiter interrupted me, probably not before time.

Yes, the Imperial Suite was available at a staggering eight guineas, and the bits-and-bobs came to six guineas. I gave him four of Ron's fivers, inviting him to keep the change, and broke the news to Phoebe that a suite included a bedroom, a bathroom and a living-room. She classed that as a house.

Ever the gent, I said she could have the bedroom and I could sleep on the sofa, which, bless her, she declared a stupid idea.

I'd just reached for her hand, when there was some kind of scuffle at the bottom of the stairs. It was bloody Eric, arguing with the head waiter. Eric brushed him aside and came over, much to Phoebe's disgust. But when he said a telegram had arrived for her, we both knew it couldn't be good news.

She wouldn't open it, so I did. Donald had been taken prisoner by the Italians. Phoebe crumpled, and Eric led her away. Her eyes were moist, and so were mine. At the bottom of the stairs she turned and gave me a little wave. Then she disappeared from my life forever.

Too upset to write more now.

. SUNDAY 20 .

When I got home, Yvonne was watching a video. She was surprised that I wasn't in Runcorn, and a bit stunned to see me wearing Reg's dinner suit. I'd forgotten about Runcorn, but it was a handy excuse to say I'd picked the suit up there, and I'd got rid of nearly all my stuff.

I must have seemed downcast, because Yvonne tried to cheer me up by saying she should have tried harder to share my interests. I told her I was

never going back . . . to Runcorn. It was just so hard to concentrate.

I'd brought the bag with the nightie in it. After all, now I'm going to spend the rest of my life with Yvonne, she deserves presents and kindness and all my attention. I'm living in the present now.

But I wanted, somehow, to tell her about Phoebe, a kind of confession without confessing. So I made up a story.

Apparently in 1940 this chap fell in love with a married woman. She loved him too but, although things weren't too good between her and her husband, she couldn't bring herself to be unfaithful to him. Until one night, when the chap booked a suite at the Savoy Hotel and bought her the nightie.

But before anything happened between them, she got a telegram to tell her that her husband had been taken prisoner, and she decided she couldn't go through with it. And she left. He went back to his wife. They took their marriage vows very seriously in those days.

While I talked, Yvonne unwrapped the tissue paper. It was a beautiful thing, négligé, or whatever you'd call it. Peach silk. Then Yvonne found the card. I'd forgotten about the card. I asked her what video she'd been watching, but she seemed puzzled. I'd scribbled the first few lines of 'Tonight' from *West Side Story*, which was written after the war. Anyway, she obviously knew my handwriting, and she took the whole thing as me being romantic, so everything was all right.

Or nearly all right, because I'd forgotten that I'd left the newsreel in the machine, and Yvonne had been watching it. There was a particular bit she wanted to show me . . .

Yvonne froze the picture. She said the brilliant young plastic surgeon was a dead ringer for me. I said I might have looked like that if I'd been around then. What else was there to say?

.MONDAY 21.

Message from Ron on the machine. Didn't call back.

.TUESDAY 22.

Ditto.

.WEDNESDAY 23.

Ron came round and virtually manhandled me out of the house and round to the pub. I made him tell me what had happened while I was away before I confessed that I hadn't bought the shares, and I'd spent a fair amount of his money. I gave him the left-over notes back, but he was inconsolable. At least I stopped him shredding them.

That's the good news. The bad news is that he never wants to see or speak to me again, and I guess I can't blame him. I'm sure I'd feel the same.

God, I'm a disaster. I've let everyone down. Eric's quite right; I've turned Phoebe's head and made her unhappy. I've made Yvonne unhappy. I've made Ron unhappy. Gary Sparrow, bringer of sunshine and happiness. I don't think.

I guess I should burn this diary, make a bonfire of my vanities, get myself together and live in the real world. Yvonne's right when she says I'm obsessive. So I suppose it's time for a new me, no obsessions. Come to think of it, no Phoebe and no Ron either.

Wonder what Christmas will be like?

DECEMBER

. SATURDAY 31 .

What a Christmas! I love my dad, but does he have to bang on every year all through the Queen's speech about how we'd be better off as a republic? And does my mum have to start dropping hints about Yvonne and me starting a family? Plus, they don't have satellite, so I missed a lot of good football.

Why am I wittering when I took this out to burn it? Why have I been sitting reading all this when I was just going to take the diary and get rid of it? Why can't I stop thinking about Phoebe and wondering how she is – and Eric, and Reg? I haven't been out East for a while, so I haven't seen the present-day Deadman. Wonder what would happen if he turned up in Cricklewood?

So. New Year resolution. Never think about any of this again. Right? Right!

But maybe I'll keep the diary after all.

APRIL 1995

.SATURDAY 1.

Well, here we are again. Back at the Dun Cow, a pint and a diary. Quite like old times. The landlord's jokes don't get any better. Fancy asking me how the train numbers were coming along.

The thing is, I don't know how I feel. I've seen Phoebe and she's changed. I'm worried about getting drawn back into all the Phoebe stuff and all the old guilt about Yvonne, but I'm not sure I can help myself. Plus, I've made it up with Ron – I think.

Yvonne's New Year resolution was to move house and have a baby, which is fair enough. I've got no strong feelings either way. I'm quite happy in Cricklewood, but if it's making her edgy, then I'd rather move just so she calms down. Not sure about the baby thing – they're okay when they reach the talking stage, but I guess you can't get ready-made ones.

A couple of weeks ago we had this really crap dinner-party – Josephine, and Magnus the mortgage broker, Mr Charisma Bypass in person. Talk about in love with the sound of his own voice. The upshot was I said I hadn't had so much fun since I fell off my bicycle, and Yvonne accused me of being a social cripple. Of course, I'm not. I just pretended I had no friends to shut her up. I mean, there's Derek and Chris at work, the guy that brings the sandwiches, the plumber who came to drain the central heating . . . Wonder why we never had that drink?

The trouble is, we're a few grand short of what we might get for Maidstone Gardens, and what we need for Maple Avenue. If it was up to me, I'd take that as a fact of life. But Yvonne wants me to see Ron, because Stella told Yvonne he had a few grand put by. She can't understand why Ron and I have had this major falling out.

I said if she didn't change the subject, I'd withdraw her conjugal rights. Instead she withdrew them. Possibly the only known case of a woman adopting the withdrawal method. I admit I'm not the world's most physical guy, but two weeks! So I went to see Ron, who gave me an extremely cool reception. I realized how much I'd missed him, but I wasn't going to tell him that.

Of course, he had me over a barrel and said I had the remedy in my own hands. All I had to do was pop back to 1941 and do the deal. I said I couldn't go back, it wouldn't be fair to start up again with Phoebe, and Eric wouldn't let me into the pub. Ron said in that case I could forget a loan and forget Maple Avenue. So I asked if he still had any of the old fivers left. After all, I was doing it for Yvonne.

I worked out a brilliant plan. There's a bank at the top of Duckett's Passage in an old building, so it seemed a fair bet it was a bank in the war. I was going to pop in and double check, when who did I meet but the modern Reg Deadman. As soon as I saw him, I knew this trip back was meant. Though I didn't know what it would mean. Don't know what it means, in fact.

I said 'Hallo,' but he didn't remember me. Unless he was pretending not to remember me.

Twenty minutes later I'd changed in the back of the van, giving my head a rather nasty bang on the roof, and I was walking down Duckett's Passage. Things had changed. Most of the street was demolished, but at least the Royal Oak was still standing.

I thought I was going to make it safely to the bank, when I bumped into the old Reg, out of uniform for once. I didn't recognize him, but he recognized me, and of course I couldn't get away. He insisted on dragging me into the Royal Oak to buy me a drink. My heart turned over, and that was it. Why have I been so dumb? Why did I stay away so long? Oh, Phoebe!

.SUNDAY 2.

The more I think about it, the more amazing it seems. Phoebe came out from behind the bar, flung her arms around me, then stepped away and called me a bastard for not writing. I'd never heard her use language like that. When an old codger complained, and she called him a silly old sod, I knew that things had moved on. I was shocked myself.

Then I said one of those things that make you go hot and cold, a little joke about not letting Eric hear her talking like that, or she'd feel the back of his hand.

Reg said the back of his hand was all they found. That, and his dentures. It was how they identified him.

I took Phoebe in my arms, muttering something sympathetic, but she pushed me away and told me not to pretend that I'd liked him. She missed him, even though he'd been a terrible old nag. Now she was running the pub on her own, with a bit of help from Reg, who was on sick leave, due to a perforated eardrum. He'd got it in the raid which did for Eric.

She then asked me the question I'd been dreading – why didn't I write? I said that after the Savoy, it seemed best to let her get on with her life. 'So, what are you doing here now?' she wanted to know.

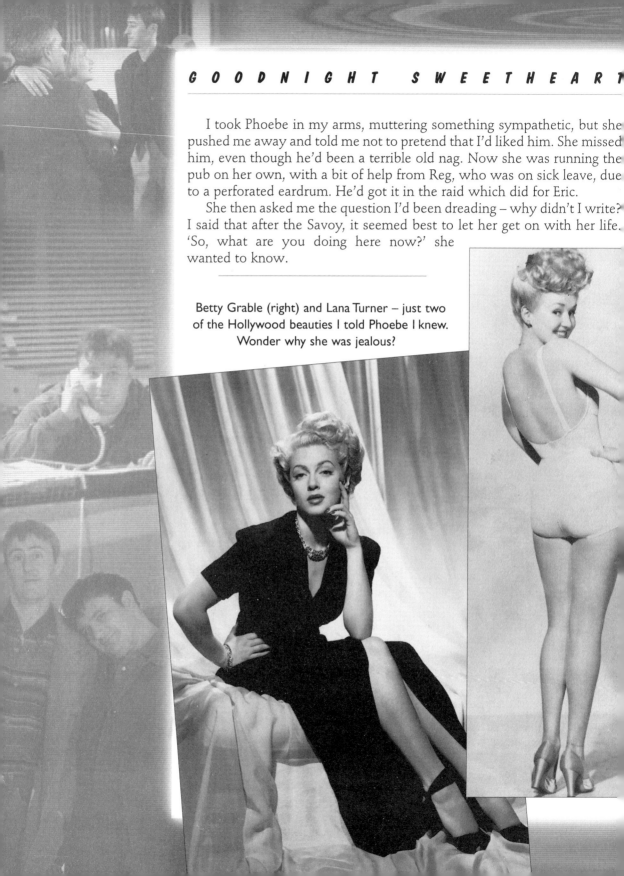

Betty Grable (right) and Lana Turner – just two of the Hollywood beauties I told Phoebe I knew. Wonder why she was jealous?

I said: 'Hollywood and I didn't really get along. It was fine to begin with, the chauffeur-driven limousine, the apartment in Beverly Hills, hob-nobbing with the stars . . . ' 'Which ones?' Phoebe asked. 'Oh,' I said, Clark Gable, Gary Cooper . . . ' 'What's he like?' Phoebe asked. 'Quiet,' I said. 'But not as quiet as Harpo Marx, of course.' 'What about the lady film stars?' Phoebe wanted to know. 'Hob nob with any of them?' 'One or two,' I said. 'Lana Turner, Betty Grable, Greta Garbo . . . More hobbing than nobbing, of course.'

Then Phoebe came out with something strange. It was as if she'd been holding herself back from me, pleased to see me but annoyed at the same time. She said, and I remember it exactly: 'You expect me to believe none of them fell for you, with those eyes that look like they've seen things other people can't even imagine?'

What a wonderful thing to say! I was all set to go on spinning tales of Hollywood when some soldiers came in, and Phoebe had to go to the bar. She started laughing and joking with them, which gave me a totally unjustified pang of jealousy. After all, I couldn't be jealous, can't be jealous. I was only there for Ron and Yvonne. I didn't even plan to go into the Royal Oak.

Reg started talking about people doing things in wartime that they wouldn't normally do, going off at a tangent about his wife and a Canadian fighter pilot. I didn't follow. He told me not to go breaking Phoebe's heart. I said I couldn't if I tried, now that she's become as tough as nails. Reg said it was all a front, but when she shouted to him to get off his backside and start collecting the pots, it seemed like a pretty convincing front to me.

I sidled off, went to the bank, and found myself in total weirdness. The assistant manager, a tall, languid, grey-haired bloke was called Wilson. And the manager, a small tubby bloke with an abrupt manner, was called Mainwaring. As Richard Littlejohn would say, you couldn't make it up.

I couldn't resist quoting 'Who do you think you are kidding, Mr Hitler?', which made Mainwaring look at me as if I was mad. Naturally, he turned out to be in the Home Guard. It was really difficult to take seriously, and being light-hearted didn't go down too well with Mainwaring. He thought there was something dodgy about my wad of cash, and was even suspicious of the new passport Ron had run up, complete with American visas and stamps. When I told him the songwriting in Hollywood bit, he was convinced I was up to no good. So, he devised a test. He whipped a music book out of his drawer, said it was the score of Handel's *Agrippina*, and asked me to hum a few bars. Well, I can do the first bit of the *Hallelujah Chorus* at a pinch, but *Agrippina*, no way. I told him the truth, that I couldn't read music.

Immediately he pressed the buzzer for Wilson, while I gabbled about Irving Berlin not being able to read music either. Wilson sauntered in; Mainwaring outlined the suspicious situation of the musically-illiterate songwriter. Wilson thought this was a real coincidence, since only the other day he'd read that Irving Berlin couldn't read music. Thank you, God.

But my troubles weren't over. Wilson suggested I should prove my story by singing one of my own songs. And my mind went a complete blank!

MONDAY 3.

Sorry, diary. I looked at the time and realized my marriage would be a complete blank if I didn't get back in time for lunch. As it was, I got: 'You spend more time in that pub than you do with me. Do you have to drink so much?'

Anyway, I remembered *My Fair Lady*, so I gave them a blast of 'I'm Getting Married in the Morning', which went down better with Wilson than with Mainwaring on the artistic front. It was Sparrow *nul points* as far as he was concerned.

We were about to start discussing shares, when a clumsy youth came in with a tray, tripped, and slopped tea into the saucers. It had to be . . . It just had to be! But I asked to make sure. And it wasn't. He wasn't called Pike, he was called Major! Perfect! If these adventures are a fantasy, if somehow I dream them or think I live them, or whatever, at least I know I've got a brilliant imagination, though I say so myself.

After that, the business didn't take long at all – 20 000 shares in Arbuthnot Brothers of Ealing, now Eurotronics Plc. Yes! I'll find out later just how much I've made when Ron and I go to see the present-day bank manager.

I bought Phoebe a brooch to celebrate and went back to the pub. It was shut, but I hammered on the door a bit and Phoebe let me in. She was wearing some kind of uniform, which turned out to be for the WVS. She said she'd tried to get into the Fannys, but you couldn't be a part-time Fanny, and they were difficult to get into. I said I knew.

She loved the brooch, but seemed really upset when I said I had to go back to America the next day. The producers wanted me to meet Judy Garland, who was up to play Eliza Dolittle.

The expression in Phoebe's eyes made me squirm; she looked like a dog when you've trod on its tail. 'I'm young,' she said. 'I'm alone, I'm lonely. My marriage was never much cop. Now I've met someone who is good, and kind, and generous, and talented, and he's going away.'

It was like treading on my own tail, or shooting myself in the foot.

Phoebe thought all those things about me, I felt everything I'd always felt for her, and I was telling her a pathetic lie. But I couldn't back down, at least not then.

When I went to see Ron, I was still pretty low, but he was quite the opposite. He reckons we've made 200 000 quid, and I've improved my bookie rating on both sides of the space-time continuum.

It's strange. Phoebe's changed. She's more passionate, more exciting. And she's still waiting for me in 1941. What am I going to do about that?

After Ron, I went home to give Yvonne the good news that the mortgage was in the bag. I pretended Ron had found me a friendly bank manager, but Yvonne couldn't come with me to meet him because it was the sort of bank that liked women to be veiled from head to toe and walk four steps behind their menfolk.

Yvonne said immediately I could forget it. She didn't want a loan from a bunch of chauvinists, thank you very much. She changed her mind when I mentioned five per cent fixed interest.

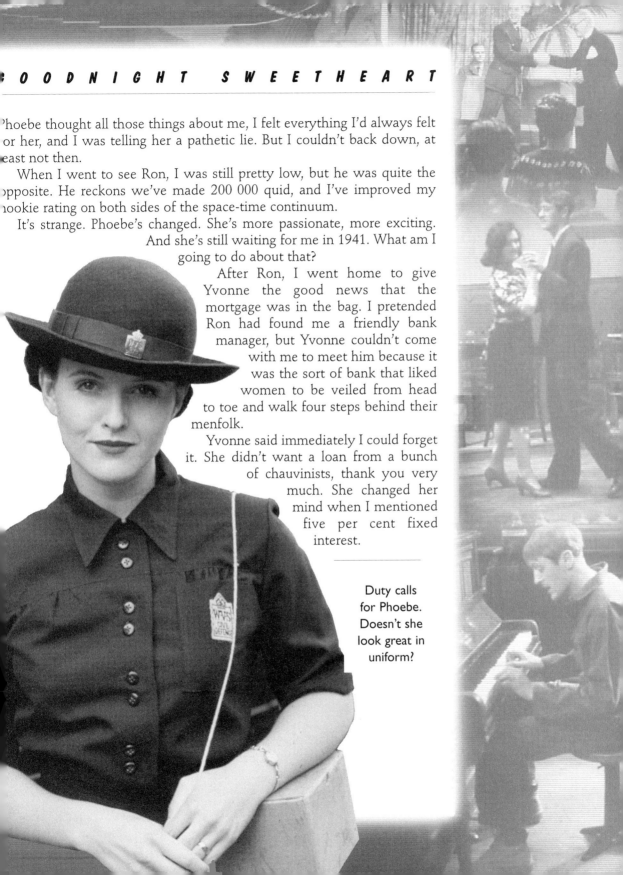

Duty calls for Phoebe. Doesn't she look great in uniform?

.TUESDAY 4.

Scribbling downstairs, Yvonne asleep upstairs.

Bollocks! Double bollocks! What a cock-up!

Went to the bank with Ron. They dug out the share certificate. Everything seemed hunky-dory. The story was that my grandfather Gareth had left me the shares in his will. When the manager got called out, I had a look at the file. Ron was kissing the share certificate, but I was more interested in a memo – a heart-sinking, gob-smacking memo.

Apparently, the Arbuthnot Brothers had a vicious bust-up in 1957 after Harold found Cecil in bed with his wife. They dissolved the partnership and set up rival companies. Harold started Arbuthnot of Ealing Ltd, and Cecil started Arbuthnot Electronics Limited.

The manager at the time couldn't trace me (bit of a surprise, that), so he had to make a decision. As a church-going man, he went for the sinned-against rather than the sinner. The problem being that Harold's company went bust, while Cecil's went on to become Eurotronics Plc.

Ron was banging his head hard on the desk when the manager came back. He assured us that Mr Major had acted from the very highest motives.

They made that shambling idiot manager!

I concocted a story for Yvonne about Mr Farouk at the Arab bank pulling out of mortgages due to a disastrous slump in the price of camels, but she didn't seem too put out. She just said she thought it was too good to be true, and that Magnus had come up with something that seemed feasible.

Goodnight, diary.

.WEDNESDAY 19.

Oh, the pressure. Pressure everywhere. Pressure, pressure, pressure.

Yvonne's still gung-ho for the move. She's writing ads for the *Standard*, putting us in n.w. Hmpstd rather than Crcklwd because it sounds better.

I do not want to move to Maple Avenue. *I do not want to move to Maple Avenue.*

Last night I was trying to say that subtly, when Yvonne ordered me to come to bed. I asked why. She said it was bedtime, and I wasn't a bat. She then said it was the most fertile day of her cycle, a fact that had, until then, escaped me, because it wasn't in my Boy Scout Diary. (I shouldn't have said diary, she might want to see it.)

Then we had the heavy chat about didn't I want to have a baby (not really feeling hungry), the Gestapo-style foreplay technique of ordering

me to drop my boxers, and the puzzled girlie stuff about didn't I like it when she took the initiative?

Not to put too fine a point on it, I couldn't put too fine a point on it. Which didn't go down well, though I'm told that's another of my failings.

THURSDAY 20.

Saw Ron for a man-to-man. Confessed that ever since Yvonne started talking about babies, I'd lost the desire to create one. Plus, if we get Maple Avenue, we'll only have about twenty quid a week left over to live on.

Ron thought my problem might be physical, but I don't fancy going to a doctor about it. I saw that programme on TV about penile implants and the one that wouldn't bend. Makes me shudder.

So Ron said why didn't I go back and see if I got a reaction with Phoebe? I tried to say that it wouldn't be fair to use her as an experiment, but Ron read my mind. He said that going back was my destiny, that I can't close the book because I haven't finished the story yet.

Sometimes, just sometimes, he talks sense.

Got back home to find Yvonne with a very pleasant couple of blokes, potential buyers. It was dog-house time, because I'd totally forgotten they were coming. She seemed very embarrassed when she said I spent more time with Ron than with her, and was I sure we weren't having an affair? It didn't click what the embarrassment was till later, and the two blokes didn't seem to mind.

One of the blokes admired my collection of blues LPs, which was nice. I think it's pretty good myself. I played him a bit of Robert 'Pete' Williams, and we talked about having a jam some time – he played bottle-neck. But his mate seemed keen to get away. It was obvious they didn't like the house.

When they left, Yvonne told me they were gay. I must say it hadn't struck me till then. You don't get many gay bottle-neck guitarists. I said so.

Yvonne started to wind me up about how well I'd got on with the bloke, that twenty per cent of married men are bisexual . . . I don't find that sort of stuff funny, and she was getting right up my nose, so rather than have yet another row I decided to leave. Yvonne wanted to know what I was doing for dinner, so I said I'd go up Colonel Sanders. She told me to be sure to take precautions. Ha, bloody ha.

On the way out, I saw her silk shirt, which she'd obviously just picked up from the dry-cleaners. I'm not sure why, but I took it.

The first person I saw when I got to the bottom of Duckett's Passage was Phoebe, giving a man on a second-hand clothes stall a hard time. I looked at her, and knew immediately my problems weren't physical. I had discovered the elusive feel-good factor.

She was surprised to see me, so I explained that the movie had been cancelled, and I'd come back to London to find I'd been bombed out. My Bechstein had been blown to smithereens. Phoebe thought it was a sausage-dog rather than a piano, and was worried in case it had suffered.

In the pub, I gave her Yvonne's shirt, which she loved. I could see her loving it. I guess I must have looked a bit smug, because she flared up suddenly, saying I couldn't turn her head that easily, and flounced off to serve some soldiers, calling them brave boys.

It's amazing what you can pick up down the market

I don't know, I get stick in the present, stick in the past. This new harder Phoebe really turns me on, but there's also a hint of Yvonne in there now.

Reg greeted me with 'Hail the conquering hero comes', which gave Phoebe an excuse to wonder where the heroism lay in writing songs. She used to like my songs! Then she called me a lounge lizard!

I thought about leaving. Instead, I went over to the piano and played her my latest composition, 'If You Leave Me Now'. I hoped the magic might be working, but when I looked in the mirror over the piano to see how the song was going down, there was Phoebe kissing a young dark bloke. I tailed the music off, but she didn't even notice.

Reg said he was called Ludo, and was foreign – a war hero. 'Unlike myself, the lily-livered lyricist,' I said bitterly. And he'd obviously thrown a six to start. Apparently, he's been in every day making a fuss of her. Did I not like that! So I went over to the bar and called for drinks all round. Stupid really, because Phoebe was totally unimpressed.

I tried chatting to Ludo, but he came over all pompous and refused to speak until we had been introduced. When he called Phoebe 'my dear', I felt like hitting the self-satisfied oily prat. He didn't like me either. She could hardly wait to take off her pinny when he asked her out for a walk.

What could I do? I got drunk and played the piano. I did 'Girl', 'Message To Martha', listened to Reg talking about his wife rolling all over the lino with half the Canadian airforce . . . Oh, we were happy!

I was giving 'You've Lost That Loving Feeling' everything I'd got, when Phoebe came back and told me to pack in the miserable wailing. Now she's starting to criticize the little things I do.

'Look, Phoebe,' I said, 'if I'm cramping your style, if I'm surplus to requirements, if you want me to sling my hook . . . ' I didn't get the answer I expected. 'Why don't you,' she said. 'What good are you doing hanging round here? Why are you?' I just burst out with it. 'Because I love you,' I said. 'Don't you feel anything for me any more?' 'I'd be lying if I said I didn't,' Phoebe admitted.

I could see her arguing with herself, saying out loud that she couldn't rely on me, but her eyes were saying something else.

I thought that telling her about my little problem becoming a big opportunity when I was with her might work, but she just said: 'Every man has that problem sometimes.' Reg said it had never happened to him. Bully for Reg!

Things warmed up a bit when I opened my case and produced the groceries – tea, coffee, sugar, butter, biscuits, steak. Phoebe looked at the label, which said Best before 22.4.95. She wanted to know what it meant.

'Um,' I said, 'they have a big military cookbook in America, written by a Colonel Sanders. And 22.4.95 is the page-number for the afters recommended by the Colonel. Turn to chapter 22, section four, find recipe 95, and it will be strawberry shortcake or something. So it's code for best before strawberry shortcake.'

She was just about to cross-examine me about the sell-by date on the coffee, when Ludo came back with some papers. It seemed he was persuading Phoebe to invest all her dad's legacy, £200, in Argentinian beef.

Maybe it was the drink, maybe a sudden flash, but a little clockwork something started whirring in my mind. Ludo, from a country in Eastern Europe over-run by the Nazis, now in the British Army . . . My mind whirred faster when I called him Ludo, and he said he wanted to be called Robert, because it sounded more English. Phoebe was helping him to find a name for after he was naturalized. She suggested Churchill. I suggested Charlton, which would go well with Bobby.

Ludo picked up the Maxwell House jar, and said that it had given him an idea. Reg thought Robert Coffee didn't sound very British, but Ludo had other ideas. Robert House, he thought, was the name for him.

I was absolutely certain that the more he thought about it, the more he would go for the other option.

But that didn't stop me trying to stop him getting his hands on Eric's pension money. I said I had about £3000 to invest myself. That got his interest all right. 'The only problem,' I said, 'is that I'll have to run the proposal past my brokers. So can I have a few details?' Ludo tried to look dignified, but blustered. When Phoebe said I might have a point, he swept up his papers and left. Good riddance to the bouncing Czech!

Phoebe was not happy. I tried to explain that if he was on the level he'd be back; and, if not, it meant he was a conman. She burst into tears and ran into the back room. I don't know. Some people just can't be saved from themselves.

Reg offered me a drink to cheer me up, so I had several, hoping that Phoebe would come back. She didn't.

Don't want to write the next bit.

.FRIDAY 21.

Here goes. Walk up the passage, get in my van. Modern Deadman appears and asks if it's my van. I tell him my name isn't Video Repairs, which seems like a good joke. I turn on the ignition. Deadman says I shouldn't do it, because he'll have to arrest me for being drunk in charge of a vehicle, and I'll lose my licence. This seems very unfair, since he has spent much of the night buying me whiskies. I

THE FIRST TASTE TELLS YOU GOOD TO THE LAST DROP

TRUST MAXWELL HOUSE to make a better INSTANT COFFEE!

1. It has the true coffee flavor and true coffee aroma you've looked for in instant coffees. And why shouldn't it have? It's all pure coffee . . . full-bodied, roaster-fresh coffee in instant form!

2. It's the world's most popular blend of coffee . . . made from your favorite Maxwell House blend! How could any other instant coffee taste so wonderful?

3. It's produced by coffee experts who have made coffee their sole profession for more than half a century . . experts who really know the fine art of coffee blending and roasting. It's Instant Maxwell House, made instantly in the cup . . . and Good to the Last Drop!

100% PURE COFFEE

Instant
MAXWELL HOUSE Coffee

Thrift Tip! A jar of Instant Maxwell House makes fully as much as a pound of regular coffee. And you make only as much as you need. No leftover coffee . . . no grounds to throw away.

tell him so. He says he'll drive me to the police station.

I phone Yvonne, and tell her a strange man wants me to get into his car. But it's all right, he's a policeman. Yvonne says something about me wearing her blouse, but the line breaks up.

I tell Deadman, truthfully, that I haven't had a drink in forty-four years.

I get into the police car. I pass out.

Oh God, please let it all be a dream.

MAY

.SATURDAY 13.

Feels like Friday the 13th – it's been a bad few weeks. Couldn't face writing. Hard enough to face Yvonne – and Ron making bad jokes. But what's new? Yvonne was half convinced I'd gone to a gay bar, half convinced I went out to get pissed to drown my sexual sorrows. All quiet on the marital front, probably because I'm sleeping in the spare room. I'm reading war books to take my mind off court on Monday, but that only makes me think of Phoebe.

Dinner with Ron and Stella tonight. She'll have the old bother boots on, no doubt, and she and Yvonne will be whispering in the kitchen, me not daring to have more than a glass of wine. God, I'm depressing myself more.

.MONDAY 15.

Another wonderful day. Thought I'd wear a tie for the court. As I was tying it, Yvonne suggested I should strangle myself. Very supportive, I'm sure. Then she predicted that, in an hour and a half, I'd be without a

driving licence and without a job. She could have pretended, just to make me feel better. I mean, I pretended that the magistrates might be ill. That one of their wives might have died, so the other magistrate took him out for dinner and they had dodgy scallops. And the court would be closed, and everything would be all right. Yvonne didn't buy it, even as a joke.

My wife and my best friend make a bet over whether I'm going to lose my licence. Thanks for your support, guys

Then Ron arrived, pretending there was a howling mob of journalists outside the door and I was on my way to death row, the long walk to the chair, all for one, one for all. Did I think he would leave me lying . . . ('Two little boys,' says Yvonne . . . And what did I want for my last meal?

What with Yvonne's ice field and the death-watch beetle hammering to get out of Ron's skull, I wondered whether I wouldn't be better off going to court on my own. But we all went.

It seemed a bit much when Yvonne bet Ron twenty quid I'd lose my licence, and he told her to make it a fiver. Naturally, he didn't pay up. Bloody Deadmen. I'll swing for them!

When we got home, I made straight for the Scotch. Well, it doesn't matter now, does it? Ron recommended caution, but what the hell. When your life

is a total botch and utter shambles, what else is there to do but get ratted?

Then my boss rang – Jackson, an oily rag in a C&A suit. 'Just a slight hiccup,' I told him, reminding him of my ten years' devoted service. He said I'd placed him in a difficult position. I said: 'I appreciate that'. He said that they couldn't afford to be a man down. I said: 'I appreciate that'. He said I could hardly do my calls on a bloody bicycle. I said: 'I fully bloody appreciate that'. He said my cards would be in the post.

'Well,' I said, 'if that's how you want to operate, there's nothing more to add. I mean, I'm a grown man. I'm not going to beg . . . ' Then I begged, but he told me I was a pathetic loser and he'd be glad to see the back of me. So I called him a fat creep and slammed the phone down.

Ron recommended some r & r in the past, but seeing Phoebe was the last thing on my mind. What was I going to do about work? What about money? When he said I could tell Yvonne I was going to work for him, I nearly kissed him. Then I nearly hit him when he said he didn't mean actually working for him. It was just something to tell Yvonne while I took stock. I told him Yvonne would be fine about it. But she wasn't. She just thrust a pile of newspapers at me and told me to start looking at the job ads. So I looked, but the top vacancy seemed to be for someone to collect the trolleys at Tesco's.

This whole episode has hit Yvonne really hard. In fact, she's talking about splitting up, which is a real shock. It makes me realize how much I depend on her, despite all the stroppiness. I've got to admit I'm not actually the most dynamic person in the world, that I do need a push sometimes. Of course, I can't tell Yvonne that, otherwise she'll never be off my case.

We had a really heavy conversation, and Yvonne went on and on. Since it was giving me a headache, I said: 'We'll talk in the morning'. But she accused me of trying to run away. I said: 'I've nowhere to run to'. Although, of course I have.

When you get as low as I've got, you deserve a bit of happiness.

.TUESDAY 16.

Bounced into the Royal Oak bright and early. Nobody around. Tapped on the counter. Up popped Reg from the cellar with a face of thunder, telling me to ring the bell and not bang on the counter. Asked for a drink. Only cherry brandy left, no beer. Great!

Phoebe arrived with some horrible piece of meat, wanting to know what I was doing there.

Then she and Reg said they wanted me to cheer them up. Honestly! Some holiday this was turning out to be. They wanted good war news. Phoebe seemed convinced we were going to lose, and nothing I could say

would persuade her we were going to win. When I said: 'I've come to be cheered up myself', she just exploded. My troubles seem crap compared with hers. I'm so selfish sometimes.

Feeling gloomy, I went to see Ron. I thought he could explain how I'd managed to screw up two lives fifty-four years apart. More fool me. Decided to make things up with Yvonne and be nice.

Went home, to find Yvonne with some woman I'd never seen before, Jenny, an old college chum. Just what I needed. When Yvonne, who was being suspiciously pleasant, offered me a beer, I said: 'No, thanks'.

'Good,' Jenny said. 'You don't want to use it as a crutch.'

That seemed a bit odd from a total stranger.

Then she started asking leading questions about whether we were a happy couple. 'Define happy,' I said. 'I suppose things have been a bit difficult lately. I've just lost my job. And, yes, there are problems. I'd be stupid not to admit it. And a lot of it is down to me I suppose. I have a tendency to run away from things. I find it difficult to face up to . . . ' I tailed off. She was taking notes! It clicked. Yvonne had sneaked in some counsellor or therapist, or whatever, under my roof! In my own home!

Naturally, I put my foot down, accusing Yvonne of ambushing me.

'Of course you've been ambushed,' she said, 'otherwise you'd never have agreed to go through with it. It's our last chance, Gary. Either we do this, or . . . '

And then she cried.

Well, I just had to try and make it better for Yvonne. I can't cope with tears. So I said: 'I'll make a real effort,' and went back to talk to Jenny.

She homed in right away on failure. Did Yvonne consider me a failure? Yvonne did, but she claimed I felt even more of a failure. I had to challenge that, but I couldn't think of anything much to prove my case.

She started asking Yvonne about herself, harking back to their time at college and old boyfriends. When Jenny mentioned Trevor Harrison, Yvonne just clammed up. Apparently, this Trevor was a bit of a train-spotter. And he wore sensible shoes. I looked on Yvonne in a new light.

But she fought back. The girl has feist. 'What about Tony Price?' she wanted to know? Then Jenny got edgy. It turned out that a bloke only had to look at her, and she was ordering a wedding dress.

Things turned nasty. There was a certain amount of screaming. Jenny fled, pursued by a flower pot hurled by Yvonne. Unfortunately, it did some damage to next door's cat, but at least it gave us something to laugh about.

Suddenly we were really close again, and it made sense to do something about it. Twice! I was a bit worried about making Yvonne pregnant, but what the hell! It really made me feel better.

.WEDNESDAY 17.

I still felt good this morning. Yvonne spoiled it a bit by saying: 'It takes more than one screw to mend a marriage'. I can never understand how women can have great sex, and still turn nasty. I was just mellow, so I thought the least I could do was share it with Phoebe. After all, I can go back when I like now. There are some advantages to being out of work.

I wanted to apologize to Phoebe, but instead she apologized to me. Looks like things are back to normal.

Two happy Sparrows
in their Cricklewood nest

JUNE

.THURSDAY 8.

Problems. Got stuck in a shelter, and couldn't remember where I'd told Yvonne I was meant to be, Basildon or Braintree. This working for Ron is a godsend in terms of cover stories, but I'll have to start remembering what they are. Definitely losing it.

I called him first thing, but no reply. I'd just put the phone down when he turned up and told me it was Cheltenham. That worried me. Ron was more worried about the fact he hadn't had an anxious phone call from Yvonne asking where I was. Plus, she'd told Stella I'd been out late every night, so it must have been on her mind.

Ron hit me with the bad news. He was going to have to fire me, because Stella thought he was working me too hard and was making him do his own ironing. I promised I'd make it clear that the hours were my responsibility. Then Yvonne came down to breakfast and really slagged him off about being a slave driver. I said it was all my responsibility, that as a salesman without a car I was at the mercy of British Rail, and I'd certainly be home early. Yvonne said that was tough, because she was going out for a drink with the girls from work.

Ron and I agreed on Reading as the destination of the day, and I headed back to the past and a date with Phoebe. I'd promised to take her to *Gone With The Wind*, which she loved. I got a lovely kiss to say thank you, and a very surprise invitation to dinner in her flat that night! No problem, Yvonne was out, and we could have a relaxed time. Checked the book – bit of a light air-raid, no casualties.

Went to have a bath, met Yvonne in the hall. She'd skipped her drinks because she realized her life was a complete and utter mess. I volunteered to fetch the evening primrose, but she said PMT wasn't the problem. It was me, my hours, the fact that I obviously didn't want to spend time with her any more.

Naturally I blamed everything on Ron. Then I made a slight error. 'How about going out for a meal soon?' I said. 'How about tonight?' she said. 'Not tonight,' I said. 'Ron wants me to work.' 'Put your foot down,' she said. So what could I do?

Luckily Ron was still in his office when I rushed round on the bike. My predicament amused him, the sod. Two women wanting me in different places at the same time was the classic adulterer's dilemma. Didn't he chortle! I explained, in a dignified way, that I was not an adulterer, and that I would never be unfaithful to Yvonne, at least not in the same space-time continuum. Though I must admit the thought of a close encounter in Phoebe's flat had not so much crossed my mind as built a nest in it.

Ron said I had to choose, a typically helpful comment. But which one? If I let Yvonne down, the marriage was over. If I let Phoebe down, she'd take it as a rejection. But to keep a date with both of them . . . Yes!

It could be done! If I took Yvonne to the Indian at the end of Duckett's passage and wore my suit, which could just about pass in the past, and kept going to the loo and was rescued by the air-raid . . .

A plan of genius, though I say so myself. Ron was impressed too, saying that if I

Outside the Indian restaurant and about to embark on an indigestible double date

pulled it off it would belong in the pantheon of man's achievements, along with landing on the moon, and making sure it was women who got pregnant.

Settling down to a starter with Yvonne.
Settling down to a starter with Phoebe.
Help!

He said he'd help. So I went for it.

Yvonne couldn't understand why I'd chosen a restaurant so far from Cricklewood, but I explained Ron had said it was both special and popular. So it was a bit of a downer when we walked in to find we were the only customers. 'Never mind,' said Yvonne, 'it'll be more romantic with just the two of us.' 'Yeah,' I said, adding: 'Ah, there's the toilet.' 'That's right, Gary,' said Yvonne, 'where it says toilet.'

She can be a bit sharp, Yvonne.

I set up the dodgy tummy alibi, and Yvonne worried about whether an Indian was the best choice, but I made reassuring noises, checking my watch while she looked at the menu. I was already running a bit late. I said: 'I'll have what you're having'.

Then the owner came over for a chat, and of all things started wittering on about publicity leaflets. Yvonne volunteered me for a quote. I was desperate to get to the bog, but the owner wanted to talk about laminated A5 brochures in full colour . . . He seemed to know more about it than me, not that I know anything about printing.

I said I'd work out the quote in the loo, then made a dash for it.

The fates were with me. There was a window. So I put my next stroke of genius into action. I'd brought my Walkman with a couple of little speakers, and a tape of me muttering, groaning and singing. No time to lose. I pressed play, crawled out the window, and found Ron where he was meant to be. He passed me a bottle of wine, and I sprinted down Duckett's Passage.

Phoebe was listening to the radio when I panted up the stairs. She didn't

seem too impressed that I was late, but she thought that wine was very posh, and liked me complimenting her on her frock, even though I confused her Eugene Wave with a French dress designer. I gulped when she showed me her stockings. What beautiful legs she has!

She sat me down and outlined the menu – M.I.5 soup ('Bet you don't know what's in it.'), plus lamb chops which she'd traded with the butcher for a cut-price barrel of beer. I knew then that tonight would have been the night, even if she hadn't said she wanted it to be special. Which she did, making me feel lousy.

I told her I'd have to keep nipping out to the call-box at the end of the street – bit of a flap on at work, etc. She wanted to know why I couldn't phone from the pub, but I said public lines were more secure.

The atmosphere had cooled a bit, and it went down several degrees more when she looked at the wine – Riesling. Only Ron, reliable Ron, the man who keeps his brains in his substantial posterior, could have bought me a bottle of German wine. Phoebe threw it away. Good start.

The clock rang the half-hour as Phoebe appeared with the soup, mock oyster, made from cods' heads and whale meat. Yummy. I wolfed it down, severely scalding the inside of my mouth, and ran for it.

It wouldn't have taken more than thirty seconds to strangle Ron, and my hands were heading for his throat when I heard distant sounds of Cliff Richard coming from the loo window in the restaurant. It meant that the tape I'd prepared earlier was finished. In my rush to get back to Yvonne, I managed to stick a foot down the lavatory bowl. I dripped my way back to the table.

The restaurant had filled up a bit in my absence, and when the food arrived Yvonne really liked it. I couldn't taste it. It was just food to be eaten as quickly as possible. At least it wasn't red hot.

Then I felt something rubbing up and down my leg, a stockinged foot, as it happens. It moved downwards and stopped. Yvonne looked puzzled.

'Gary,' she asked, 'why is one of your feet soaking wet?'

Naturally, after an awkward pause for thought, I had the perfect explanation. 'Well,' I said, 'I filled up the hand-basin in the gents to wash my hands, put my foot up on it to tie my lace, and it slipped and fell in. You've never done that?'

She was about to answer when, thank heaven, the owner came over and Yvonne reminded me about the printing quote. I whipped out a notebook, scribbled some figures in a despairing attempt to make them look good, tore out the page and handed it over. He said: 'You have to

SIMPLE DISHES FOR WAR-TIME

be joking,' so I knocked fifty pounds off.

Damn! He thought I was joking because the quote was too low, not too high. He was so happy that he called for free seconds of chicken tikka for us. I tried very hard to look grateful, while Yvonne told me not to look a gift course in the mouth.

Climbing back through the window was a bit of a struggle. It felt as if a large weight had been clamped to my stomach. Phoebe had done us lamb chops, peas and potatoes, and insisted I clear my plate. Wasting food was as good as giving it to Adolf. Oh, what a struggle!

I did my call-box routine again, to a Phoebe who was growing increasingly irritated, then made a careful re-entry through the window, avoiding the bowl. Ron had nodded off.

It struck me that, instead of ranking with man's highest achievements, this double date was the product of a diseased imagination.

As I picked at my mutton vindaloo – why had I ordered mutton vindaloo? – I felt quite bilious. 'Are you bulimic or pregnant?' Yvonne wanted to know. 'Yum, yum,' I said, and somehow finished it, despite a faintly embarrassing moment when my stomach made its own comment on the proceedings, and Yvonne asked if the restaurant was over the tube.

While Yvonne was getting crosser, Phoebe had obviously decided to make the best of things. When I got back for suet pudding (suet pudding!), she'd turned off one of the lights and found some sweet music on the wireless. As I grimly attacked the pudding, she said she wanted every night to be like that.

I couldn't really speak, but I hope she took my mumble as agreement.

It wasn't so much a run as a stagger back up the passage to the present. I woke Ron up to tell him I was having a coronary, but it didn't seem to register. I said it was time to put Plan B into operation, and he

should come into the restaurant in five minutes. Ron wasn't clear about Plan B, but that's because I hadn't explained it to him.

Yvonne was extraordinarily stroppy when I got back, for which I couldn't really blame her. She demanded that I get the bill. I said: 'I want coffee and a hot flannel, and I won't be going to the loo again.' She snapped that I shouldn't need to go again for a fortnight, and the few minutes we'd spent together had been nice.

Then Ron arrived. Poor old Ron. He wasn't at all prepared for my attack about how he had followed us to the restaurant with his business obsession, and how I was going to teach him to leave me in peace.

I pushed him out the door. At first he was thrilled with the brilliance of Plan B. Then he realized I'd made him look a total git.

Phoebe was also extraordinarily stroppy when I got back to her. I couldn't really blame her either. She was clearing the table, and wondered sarkily if I could spare the time when I offered to help. 'I don't believe that there's a flap at work,' she said. 'You sure that's not just been an excuse?' 'For what?' I wanted to know. 'Avoiding me,' she said. 'I wanted us to spend the night together tonight . . .'

So it was true. We could have had our first night together, a whole night! Sod it, sod it, sod it! All I could do was explain about the raid, and she still looked dubious, until the sirens went. Then she hugged me and apologized, which did nothing at all to make me feel any better.

Ron grabbed me on the way back to the restaurant. Yvonne had phoned Stella to complain about him, Stella had phoned Ron to tell him he was a bastard, but he still wished me well. He's a true mate, Ron Wheatcroft. I'm sure he'll find a way out of the restaurant leaflet problem. I didn't have the heart to tell him there and then.

My stomach was a good excuse for sleeping in the spare room. I lay awake all night, thinking about Yvonne, thinking about Phoebe, wondering if I was any good to either of them.

. TUESDAY 13 .

Got home from the library to hear an explosion and find Yvonne waving a bottle of Champagne. I thought immediately she was pregnant, and said so, which ruined the atmosphere. Instead, it turns out she's been promoted to assistant personal manager. What a relief! It sounds really good – more money, her own office, seat in the executive dining room . . . I suggested popping out to celebrate. As we were leaving, the phone rang, but Yvonne said to ignore it. The

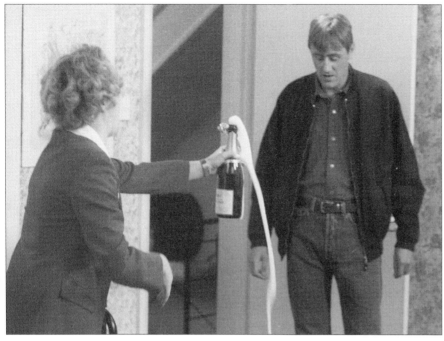

Yvonne pops her cork and gets Champagne all over the carpet

answering machine kicked in, and there was Stella, wondering how I'd taken the news that the new job was in Macclesfield.

I was stunned. Yvonne didn't seem at all put out. We'd just have to move. I wondered when she'd been planning to tell me – as the furniture was being packed into the van?

She just couldn't understand why I was so against it, and I couldn't really say, 'Well, because I'm a time-traveller and I like to nip back to the past now and then'. So I took refuge in my parents and not wanting to be too far away from them.

Then, as usual, it got a bit personal. Yvonne said we were talking about her career. I said: 'What about my career?' She said if we moved to Macclesfield, I might be able to get one, which was really below the belt, one of the worst things she's ever said to me.

I pretended that Ron was about to make me Head of Marketing Development, though I had to admit it would be a department of one, albeit with my own rubber plant, but she brushed that aside. She was going up for a few days to check the place out, and why didn't I come with her? I told her that, under no circumstances, was I prepared to move and went off to the Dun Cow by myself.

.WEDNESDAY 14.

Relations still cool. Irresistible force meeting immovable object.

.FRIDAY 16.

Popped back to see Phoebe, but she was organizing stuff for a party in the pub, and didn't really have time to chat. Since I felt like hell, I wasn't very good company, so I popped back to the present again. I only want her to see me when I'm on top of my form. I always want things to be perfect. If I turn into a grumbling git, she might not fancy me any more.

Went to see Ron and whinged to him instead about the old, old problem. Why was I putting wanting to see Phoebe ahead of supporting Yvonne?

Ron said it was Friday. On Fridays I felt guilty about Yvonne. I'd spend the weekend with her, clear my conscience, then feel bad about Phoebe on Monday, and start the cycle all over again.

I was stunned. Am I so predictable? Guess I am. Ron threw me by saying that his staff set their watches by me. Turns out they know I have two women in my life. The men give me serious respect. But, Ron said, I shouldn't accept coffee from any of his female staff.

Then I made a momentous decision, the biggest decision I've ever made in my life. I'm going to commit myself to one girl. I'm going to return to a time when I might be of some use, to an age where British men and women stood shoulder to shoulder facing the bombs and bullets. Once Yvonne has gone to Macclesfield, I'm going to leave my clothes on a bridge, fake my own suicide and disappear.

I told Ron. He thought I was joking. But I wasn't, and I'm not. After all, Yvonne doesn't need me, I realize that now. She can make her own way in the world. I just hold her back.

No, I'm going to live in the past, marry Phoebe and run the Royal Oak. Yvonne goes to Macclesfield on Monday. That gives me time to plan. I have never been so serious about anything in my life. But I need Ron's help, and he doesn't want to give it.

.SATURDAY 17.

Several drinks with Ron. Think he's weakening. Yvonne still trying to persuade me to come with her. Looking at her with new eyes. She seems like a stranger, but a stranger I've lived with for five years. She's beautiful sometimes. Must do some stuff in the house before I disappear.

.SUNDAY 18.

Fantastic DIY day. Fixed the kitchen shelves after months of nagging. Put a bottle of Chablis in the fridge for when she gets back. I'll miss her. Wonder how long it'll take for her to get over me? A week? Am I doing the right thing? Yes.

.MONDAY 19.

Such a sad morning. Kept telling Yvonne I loved her. She didn't really understand, but how could she? She thought I was trying to make up for rejecting Macclesfield, which made it sadder. I said that nothing could stop her now, that she was simply the best. I couldn't stop my eyes filling with tears, even when I told her that I'd be in Scotland for Ron, so not to bother phoning.

I wanted to say something really deep and meaningful, something to sum up all the best bits of our relationship. And there have been good bits – there really have. Lots of good bits.

All I could say as I watched her walk down the path was goodbye.

I went back into the house and wandered around a bit. It's a horrible house, really, so small and pokey, such a horrible colour scheme in the sitting room. I can't think why I never changed it.

But I was determined. I packed some stuff for 1941 in a case, wrote a brief suicide note (Goodbye cruel world. Gary Sparrow), then I watched some videos. There won't be any videos where I'm going. I won't miss them at all.

.TUESDAY 20.

Ron came round at 6 a.m., to drive me to Southwark Bridge and my new life. It was a very stilted conversation, not a time for jokes. I asked him to keep an eye on Yvonne for me, and he said I could do that myself. It was too late for that kind of discussion. He said he'd miss having a time-travelling mate.

We were both getting quite emotional, so I cut it short. He wished me a nice death. I wished him all the best. Then he drove off before I realized I only had wartime money in my wallet, and I couldn't pay for the tube. Bugger!

There was nothing for it but to walk. I left my suicide note with my modern clothes in a plastic bag, picked up the case and set off on my long walk.

By the time I got to the Royal Oak I was totally and utterly knackered. Even Reg noticed. I said I'd walked all the way from Southwark, and he told me I should have taken a bus. He used to know all the bus routes, but since the information could be invaluable to the Hun, he'd trained himself to forget everything he ever knew. In fact, he's aiming to get to the stage where he knows nothing of any interest whatsoever.

Fond as I am of Reg, I'm not relishing the prospect of having deep and meaningful conversations with him on a daily basis.

Me and Mrs Bloss, not one of the world's most undertstanding landladies when it comes to female visitors

Phoebe spotted the suitcase and came over. 'You're not going away again, are you?' she asked? 'Yeah,' I said, 'I'm moving on. I've said goodbye to Crickle-wood for ever.' 'So,' Phoebe said, 'now it's my turn for the brush-off, is it?' 'It'd be a bit stupid of me, seeing as I'm planning to move in around here,' I said.

She gave me a big hug. Then, practical, she wanted to know where I was planning to stay. It was important for the suggestion to come from her rather than me, but she made it immediately. Why didn't I rent the room upstairs. Naturally, I said the thought had never crossed my mind, but Phoebe can read me like a book.

Reg had to stick his oar in of course, saying he knew someone with a couple of rooms to rent. I said: 'I'll be fine at the Royal Oak.' But he wouldn't have it. Living there with Phoebe wouldn't be seemly, if I didn't mind him saying so. I did, and told him.

Then Phoebe took his side, which was a bit of a bummer. My plans seemed to be unravelling a bit. On the other hand, Reg said the rooms were just around the corner in Ravenscroft Street, which didn't seem so bad. They belonged to a lady friend, so Phoebe teased him a bit. She didn't know he had any lady friends.

Reg went pink, and said she was strictly a professional acquaintance, although she occasionally buffed up his helmet.

I've always been crap at keeping a poker face, and Phoebe saw that I was disappointed, so she tried to cheer me up. Reg was thrilled, and took me round straight away to meet his friend, Mrs Bloss. She runs a hat shop downstairs, Maison Bloss, and she seems okay in a landlady-ish sort of way. Lots of rules. I tried a bit of charm, but she seems to want to keep herself to herself, which suits me. I'm paying the huge sum of seven shillings and sixpence a week!

The rooms are, well . . . they're rooms. There's a big old bed with a chamber pot underneath, a couple of chairs where you can feel the springs . . . It's all heavy and dark, like my gran's furniture, really. It does feel so strange to be here. I can't quite believe it. Wonder how Yvonne's getting on? No, I don't want to wonder that. I'm here, and that's it. Think I'll go for a wander to orient myself, then pop in to see Phoebe.

.WEDNESDAY 21.

Went out shopping for food. Phoebe came round to inspect the premises. She really likes the place. I pulled down the blackout to show how good it was, but she said that was a sign of hanky-panky and did I want to get her talked about? So I let it up again, and we went to look at the kitchen. When she saw the mangle, it was a huge source of excitement. Other women might go into ecstasies over a diamond. For Phoebe, it's a mangle.

She wasn't so impressed with my shopping – some really horrible bacon. She told me I had to get to know the butcher, and then I'd have access to under-the-counter stuff. 'But what about your American contacts?' she asked. I said: 'They're now ruled out for security reasons.' I hadn't really thought about the food problem, but I did then and I'm thinking about it now. How did people survive? Oh well, I'll get used to it.

We were just getting down to a snog when there was a knocking at the door. It was Mrs Bloss, reminding me that there was a rule against having

young ladies in my room. I said: 'I already have one.' Mrs Bloss said darkly that she could hear everything that went on, which spoiled the atmosphere, but, anyway, Phoebe had to go off to the WVS. When she left, I did some heavy bouncing on the bed. Boy, do those springs creak! If Phoebe and I . . . when Phoebe and I finally get it together, it'll sound like the charge of the Light Brigade.

A fun night out at the movies. Phoebe blowing raspberries at Hitler isn't my idea of ladylike

Anyway, my bouncing had the desired effect. La Bloss gave her ceiling a good hammering with a stick of some kind. Nosy old cow.

.THURSDAY 22.

What a day! I was so knackered my first night I slept like a log. But, last night, wherever I turned, I seemed to find a spring. When I finally nodded off, I was woken up by some appalling clattering in the street, which turned out to be the milkman with two whacking great churns on the back of a horse-drawn cart. The up-side is it's like living in history. The down-side is that it's so bloody uncomfortable.

I went out to do the shops, and spent four hours wandering round looking for razor blades with total lack of success. At least one of the shops must have them – they're just keeping them for their regulars.

And the queues! There were queues for everything. It was like Moscow, where people saw a queue and stood in it just in case it was for something good. There are gaping holes where buildings used to be, the park's been turned into allotments, everything seems dingy somehow – dingy and small.

Odd how I only just seem to have noticed. Before it was down the passage, into the pub, be with Phoebe ... Okay, we've been out a bit, but I suppose I was wearing a large pair of rose-coloured spectacles.

I'll get used to it, I know I will.

I'll never work out why George Formby is so popular with everybody. I've always hated him

LONDON, THURSDAY, JUNE 22, 1941

AIR ATTACK ON LONDON RENEWED LAST NIGHT

1,374 NAZIS DOWN IN FIRST MONTH

Saturday marked the end of the first month of mass air raids on Britain, during which the Germans lost 1,374 machines. The R.A.F. losses in the same period were 407 'planes, the pilots of 213 being safe.

Yesterday's figures, based on reports up to 8 p.m., were eight enemy and three British 'planes down, one R.A.F. pilot being safe. Later reports will no doubt show an increase in German 'planes destroyed.

The losses on Saturday were 99 Nazi machines to 22 R.A.F. 'planes, nine of our pilots being safe. The Air Ministry announced yesterday that 46 enemy aircraft are now known to have been shot down on Friday and that 12 instead of 10 of our pilots are safe.

Following are the weekly losses on both sides:

Week ended	German	British
Aug. 17	492	115 (46 safe)
" 24	243	51 (30 safe)
" 31	296	113 (70 safe)
Saturday	343	128 (71 safe)

NEW TACTICS IN BIG ATTACK ON DOCKS

SIX FIGHTERS TO EACH BOMBER
BY OUR AIR CORRESPONDENT

In the attack on the Docks area

PERSONAL DIRECTION BY GOERING

DOCK TARGETS MISSED IN FIRST BIG RAID

HOUSES HIT: MANY FIRES: 1,700 KILLED AND INJURED

The big air attack on London, which began with a mass daylight raid on Saturday evening and continued during the night, was resumed last night, when the warning was given at 7.59 as dusk fell.

Goering, creator of the German Air Force, is directing the attack. He said in a broadcast yesterday from his headquarters in Northern France that he could see waves of 'planes headed for England.

He did not mention the price which the raiders paid, though the German radio had admitted "great sacrifices."

These were disclosed in a British official statement last night, which showed that on Saturday the Germans lost 99 'planes, or more than one in

Of these, anti-aircr...

21. The R.A.F. lost 22... pilots of nine are safe.

A scene of desolation in a London ... incendiary bor ...

"BRITISH PEOPLE OUT TO THI

FROM OUR OWN COR.
NEW Y

The calm behaviour of ... under the worst aerial poun ... impressed upon American ... ever that Britain cannot be ... One simply cannot p...

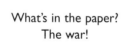

What's in the paper?
The war!

Then we went to the movies. What a disaster! Phoebe started blowing raspberries at Hitler on the newsreel, which was really embarrassing and not very ladylike. Then we were just having a snog when Reg interrupted by asking whether I was all right for fire-watching duty tomorrow. As a local resident, I'm apparently on some kind of rota. Can't say I like the sound of it. But Phoebe seemed to expect me to be keen about doing my bit, so I pretended to be enthusiastic.

Then the killer blow: an announcement that *Lady Hamilton* was being replaced as the main feature by *Turned Out Nice Again*, starring George Formby.

I realize that I haven't mentioned George so far. I know why. Because I hate him. I've always hated him. I hate his horrible whining voice, his plunking ukulele, his self-satisfied smirk that I'd like to put a fist into. The first time I saw him I felt sick. I feel sick now.

But Phoebe's a fan. I wanted her to leave, but she wouldn't. I asked her to come back here, but she's on duty.

We've had a row – our first real row! All my fault, of course. I don't know why I do this, but sometimes I just get grumpy and grudging, and

Reg makes himself at home when I'd rather he was in his own home

something inside turns me into a miserable bastard. So I stormed out, I couldn't help myself. How can I make it up with her?

Mrs B was on the way out as I was coming in. Said she was going to the pictures. Bet she's a big fan of George, too.

God, I'm so bored! The only interesting thing was when I looked out the window, and an ARP warden told me to put the light out.

As for the paper! There's the war, the war. George Formby and the war. Great! Plus, it's the Test Match on TV. I can just imagine watching it with half-a-dozen cans of beer and a seven-dish Chinese. I am so hungry! There's only one thing not on ration, and I'm not getting any of that either. And, now, there's a knock on the door . . .

It was Phoebe! She wanted to make it up with me! We both apologized. She said she was nervous of Mrs B interrupting again, but I knew she was at the pictures. So I started wondering whether Phoebe would think it too unconventional to use a chair, rather than the bed, when there was another knock on the door. Bloody Reg!

Phoebe flew into a panic about not wanting him to find her there, so I told her to hide under the bed while I got rid of him. Reg was being kind really, but what a moment to choose.

He didn't want me to feel lonely, and wondered if I'd like to go dancing. I told him he wasn't my type, edging him towards the door, but he pushed past me and sat down, taking out his pipe. He was settling in

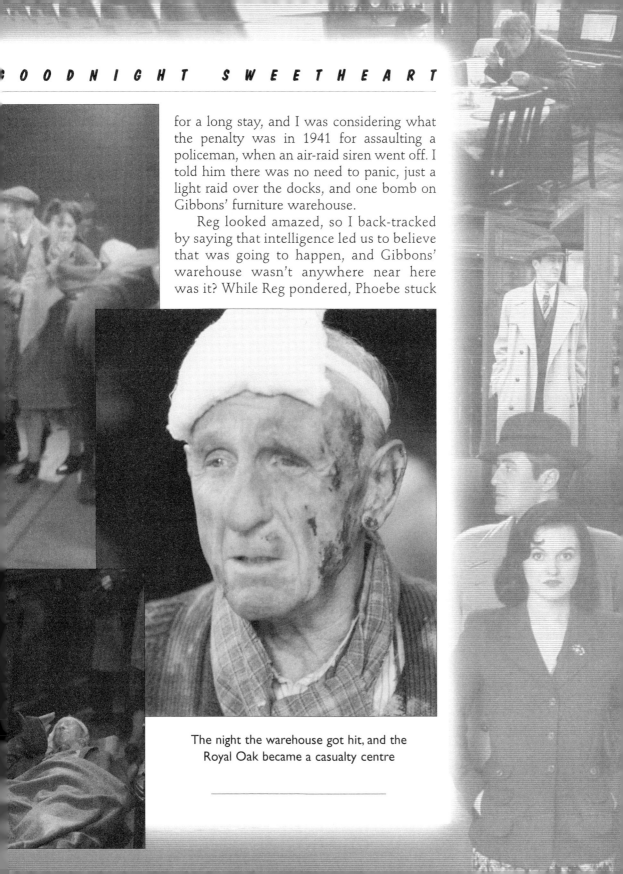

for a long stay, and I was considering what the penalty was in 1941 for assaulting a policeman, when an air-raid siren went off. I told him there was no need to panic, just a light raid over the docks, and one bomb on Gibbons' furniture warehouse.

Reg looked amazed, so I back-tracked by saying that intelligence led us to believe that was going to happen, and Gibbons' warehouse wasn't anywhere near here was it? While Reg pondered, Phoebe stuck

The night the warehouse got hit, and the Royal Oak became a casualty centre

her head out from under the bed and said: 'It's just around the corner' We joined her under the bed just as the building shook from a very loud explosion.

We lay there, cramped, sneezing and manoeuvring the chamber po without liking to mention it, until the all-clear went. Reg rushed off and Phoebe told me to come with her and make myself useful.

It was horrible. It's one thing to see pictures, quite another to be dragging injured people out of a building, to hear the screaming and the pleading and the groans.

Everyone was amazing. At the time, I suppose I was pretty good but there wasn't really any time to think. Phoebe told me what to do and I did it.

The pub was turned into a casualty centre, and we helped the wounded in there. Phoebe asked if I knew how to bandage a fractured jaw. When I said 'No', she told me to help a woman struggling with one end of a stretcher. I took over, and we laid the stretcher down. The injured guy groaned, and, as I tidied his blanket, I saw something horrible – a gap where one of his legs should have been.

When he asked me whether it was bad, I just couldn't lie. I told him he'd lost his leg. 'Not another one,' the man said. Turned out he'd go pissed five years ago, fallen down a coal-hole, and lost it that way.

I wandered over to Reg, who was trying to cheer up one bloke who was particularly badly injured. It turns out that he'd been up on a roof fire-watching. Which is what I'm down for tomorrow night. I just don' think I can face it. I know I can't face it. Guess I should try to sleep.

FRIDAY 23.

Didn't sleep. Phoebe came round first thing to tell me the water was of because a bomb hit the main, but Reg had been to the standpipe, and there was water at the pub. Great!

Then Mrs B started shouting for me, so I pushed Phoebe into the kitchen and told her to pretend there was no one there. Instead of going away, Mrs B came in and started nosing through my drawers. I gave her a moment or two, then wished her good morning. Mrs B was a bit put out but rallied quickly with a crack about Phoebe being there early. Then, a Phoebe left, she started talking about last night, and one of the fire watchers' heads being blown off. What should she do with my belonging if my head was blown off? 'Please!' I told her. 'Feel free to give my ha away.' But she kept nagging. Boy, does she get on my nerves!

Was Phoebe my next of kin, she wanted to know, and was I a friend of her husband's too? So I told her Phoebe and I were lovers, up to sexua aerobics morning, noon and night. That got rid of her! I slammed the door with a great feeling of satisfaction, tried to fry up some of the crap bacon for breakfast, threw it out and went in search of food.

After walking for what felt like hours, and probably was, I found a café that could do me some watery tea from an urn and a piece of toast. What a banquet! This 1940s lark is wearing a bit thin, I must say. I had visions of tucking myself up in the Royal Oak with Phoebe every night, doing a bit of light pint-pulling. And what's the reality? No food, no telly, no decent papers, and George sodding Formby!

As for the fire-watching, I came up with a plan. So I hobbled into the Royal Oak with a very pronounced limp. Reg said I couldn't walk around on a roof all night with my leg in that condition, which was music to my ears. No, he said, they'd have to get me a chair. Marvellous!

Back to the present for a dish of humble pie with Ron

Phoebe came out from the back room, told me she wanted to speak to me immediately, and took me into the snug. What was I doing telling Mrs Bloss that we did sexy acrobatics? Didn't I know she was a married woman? What was I trying to do to her?

I said weakly: 'I didn't think you cared what people thought.'

Phoebe, quite rightly, said: 'There's a difference between people thinking something's going on, and telling them that it is.' Apparently, Mrs Bloss shared the news with the whole queue at the fishmonger's. If someone told the brewery, Phoebe could lose her licence.

Just one bloody thing after another! I apologized. Phoebe accepted my apology. When she said she was looking forward to lunch, my spirits rose. But it was a cheese sandwich, and there wasn't any for me. I slumped again. She wanted to know my plans for the day. I said: 'I don't have any, apart from hanging around.' 'Don't you have to go to work?' I pretended I was on leave. Phoebe was unimpressed. And when she and Reg started a long discussion about the Duke of Windsor and the abdication crisis, I felt

like a fish out of water. There was nothing I could contribute. Phoebe called me a Gloomy Gus, and she was right.

I don't know where I belong. I don't know what I want. I just seem to have a great gift for taking something good and destroying it. If only I could talk to Ron.

Well, I did talk to Ron. I knew that using my plastic to get 1990s money would blow the suicide story away, but what could I do? I had to eat. Food, real food!

I went to the hole in the wall, then headed for the café at the top of the passage and, blow me down, there was Ron reading a paper and looking as if he'd always known I was going to materialize opposite him at that precise moment. He was as smug as ever, but for once I couldn't blame him. If I'd thought about it properly, I'd have known I couldn't really survive in the past full time. Why couldn't I have just been happy flitting between two eras?

Ron did a bit of a wind-up, telling me that Yvonne had been devastated for five minutes, then got involved with Les at work, who I know fancies her. He kept me hanging on in agony before he said that the suicide note hadn't been found, and as far as Yvonne was concerned I was still in Inverness. A tramp must have taken the clothes, though he would have to be a particularly unfussy tramp.

Amazing! I was prepared to do the honourable thing, commit to one girl, but it's like I'm being told it's okay to go on as I have been.

Ron said Yvonne's job in Macclesfield didn't work out, and I felt sorry for her. But then the waitress arrived, and I couldn't restrain myself. I ordered a feast of double egg, chips, beans, double bacon, double sausage, another egg, mushrooms, tomatoes, double bubble, two rounds of toast and a tea. Magic! The waitress looked surprised. Ron explained that I'd been in Scotland.

And so, wiping the egg off my chin, I got Ron to give me a lift home, looking forward to a tender moment with Yvonne. Instead I found her in hyper mode, demanding to know where I'd been and why I hadn't phoned. When I sympathized with her about Macclesfield, she wanted to know how I knew. 'Ron,' I said.

It turns out that, yet again, Ron offered sympathy which Yvonne took for a pass. How does he do it? Perhaps because he never uses one word when ten will do. I changed the subject to Macclesfield. The job turned out to be dead-men's shoes, and Yvonne thought Macclesfield was a dead-and-alive hole. When she mentioned our penchant for a little light S&M, over lunch with her future colleagues, they looked at her as if she was Madame Cyn.

That gave me an idea. Yvonne thought it was a good idea. Be it ever so small and pokey, there's still no place like home!

.SATURDAY 24.

Bounced into the Royal Oak with a cheery smile and a collection of goodies – stockings, food . . . But they weren't received with the usual warm gratitude. Reg said I was getting a reputation as a black-marketeer, and Phoebe wanted to know why I'd missed my fire-watching duty. I said: 'I had an unexpected call to work,' but Reg lost his temper and used the 'F' word, saying: 'It isn't flaming good enough'. Phoebe said: 'You could have let them know. Old Norman was pulled out of his sick bed to cover for you.' Plus: 'People are saying you didn't turn up because you were frightened.'

Well, after a great dinner, and a great night, and a great breakfast, what could I do but volunteer my services for tonight?

Pity there's going to be a big raid. Help!

.MONDAY 26.

I've got to write this down, got to write it down, got to write it down. My hand's shaking. Concentrate Gary, concentrate.

We went up on the roof, me and Phoebe and Reg, Stan and Bob. The fire-watchers.

A warehouse. A paint warehouse! I felt like Joan of Arc. Seven floors of paint and turps and thinners, and the most up-to-date fire-fighting equipment – a tin helmet and a bucket of sand.

Phoebe recalled Eric's view that you'd be better off sticking your head in the sand and using your tin hat to cover your arse. Probably the most sensible thing Eric ever said.

Reg asked me: 'What shouldn't be done with a burning incendiary bomb?' Of course, I didn't have the faintest idea. 'Never throw them at animals or put them in your pocket?' Reg said that wasn't quite the answer he'd been expecting. In fact, one should never put them in water, because they'd flare up and explode.

Reg allocated patrolling stations, leaving me and Phoebe with the roof to look after. I wasn't sure whether that was good news or bad. Whatever, I tried to make the best of it. 'Nice night,' I said to Phoebe. 'Bomber's moon,' she replied. 'What, out of plane windows?' I asked. She didn't get the joke.

So we had a cup of tea from her thermos and settled down against a

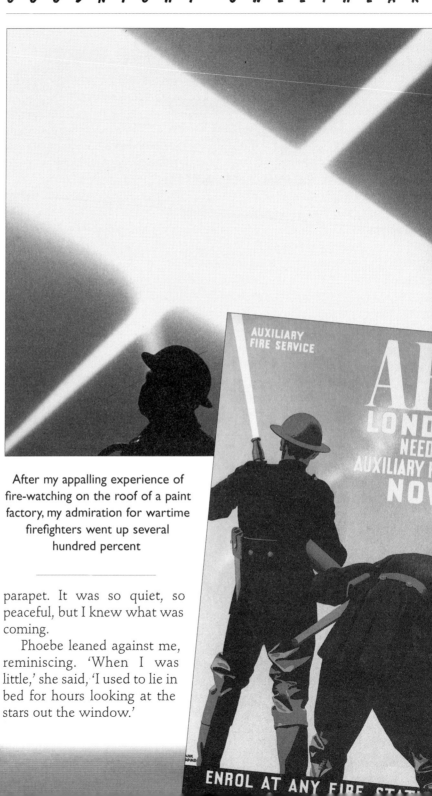

After my appalling experience of fire-watching on the roof of a paint factory, my admiration for wartime firefighters went up several hundred percent

parapet. It was so quiet, so peaceful, but I knew what was coming.

Phoebe leaned against me, reminiscing. 'When I was little,' she said, 'I used to lie in bed for hours looking at the stars out the window.'

That made her think of the family, and the big Sunday dinners they all used to have at her Aunty Dot's, sitting round the big wooden table. It was the table that saved her when the bomb fell on the house next door. Stout British oak. Not from IKEA then.

She sat occupied with her thoughts. I didn't feel like talking. The air-raid siren came in bang on cue. Phoebe huddled closer, saying she always felt okay when she was with me.

I could hear the planes getting closer and closer, see the ack-ack fire in the sky. I was gripped in a dream and I couldn't wake up. Then I saw lights in the street – flashes. Phoebe said they were incendiaries. There were hundreds of them! Something plopped on the roof, fizzing and flashing. I froze, until Phoebe told me to get the sand on it. Then the adrenaline started pumping, and I dashed over with the bucket. Another one landed. I ran over there – more sand. I was doing it. I was putting them out! It was better than sex!

A heavy explosion brought me back to reality. Phoebe said it was time to go down, but I was insane. I said: 'I'll stay on the roof in case there are more incendiaries,' and tried to get her to leave. But she said: 'If you're staying, I'm staying.'

So we held hands and crouched by the door, which seemed to offer some kind of shelter. The noise was incredible, the air was hot. Phoebe was trembling. I'm sure I was, too.

She asked me to sing her one of my songs. Good old Gary, a song for every occasion. What else could it be but 'Up On The Roof'? I know I've sung better. I don't think it was written for a trembling voice. But I did my best, until an explosion seemed to crack my eardrums and we were both flung face downwards with the force of it.

After that, there was no more singing. Phoebe was so shocked that she didn't notice me gibbering, thank God. I was so concerned to look after her that I didn't notice the effect on me.

The raid stopped after what seemed like an eternity. I took her back to the pub, felt a tiny bit better when she said I'd been fantastic up there, then came home. Trouble was, I couldn't stop the trembling. I told Yvonne I'd got the flu and I'd be up to bed when I'd made myself a hot drink.

I sat on the sofa, cuddling a cushion and shaking and shaking. I haven't really stopped since. I'm not brave. But Phoebe and Reg are. I love her so much. I must be nicer to her. I must stop shaking.

THURSDAY 29

Only shaking at night now, though I've started scratching. Can't stop the dreams of going up in flames while Phoebe and Reg dance around, throwing buckets of water over me and singing Arthur Brown's 'Fire'.

Yvonne has a new enthusiasm for getting us together – acting. Don't know whether to be pleased or not that Macclesfield fell through, because it means that she's putting all her energies into us. The Willesden Wildeans, would you believe? I've always had a sneaking feeling that I've got a touch of the Sean Beans about me. I've certainly got a better bum. So it's audition time.

Went to see Ron to clear up a little domestic problem which has been forcibly drawn to my attention. To wit, why has Yvonne never seen me with a pay cheque? Given that it's the end of the month tomorrow, it would be nice to show her one. Ron said: 'The best way to lose a friend is to lend him money.' I said: 'The best way to lose a friend is not to lend him money.' I phoned directory enquiries to find a number for the Sally Army homeless hostel to emphasize the point. He paid up, grudgingly. Then said the only production I could appear in was *The Idiot*.

FRIDAY 30

Bloody theatricals! As camp as a row of tents, with egos the size of Everest. Plus it's the most appalling play. Total waste of bloody time.

Yvonne's audition was great. She gave it her all, while I lurked about making encouraging noises and scratching a bit. Must be some sort of nervous reaction, unless the Luftwaffe dropped itching powder bombs that never made the history books.

I've got Yvonne's script here. I must write some of this down.

This is Priscilla speaking (i.e., Yvonne): 'You can't go! You can't go now! You can't leave me, no money, no future, five months' pregnant!' (Falls to her knees). 'What do you want me to do? To beg? To scream? To kill myself?

Gregory and I fall out at the Willesden Wildeans

Because this time I won't fail. This time it won't just be an overdose, a cry for help! This time it's the razor, Justin! You want to be a great film director! You want to have final cut!! Well, here it is!!!' (Slashes her throat, then falls to the floor, a gush of blood shooting into the air).

She gave it some real welly, and they loved it. The director, Gregory, who also wrote the garbage, said she had brought his play to life and offered her the part on the spot. Well done Yvonne!

I let the applause die down a bit, then asked about Justin, the male lead. This provoked some theatrical laughter and waving of arms. Lance, an ageing juvenile in lycra shorts with what looked like a cucumber poked down them was really patronizing. He told me he was already cast as Justin. Gregory said: 'Nobody handles leading parts like Lance.' I'll bet.

Like an idiot, I asked for a chance to read anyway. Lance got on his high horse and quoted me his CV – a member of the BBC radio repertory company, and a small part in *Trainer*. That must have inspired the cucumber.

Gregory soothed me down by saying I could play the pivotal role of Police Constable Barr. I'd have one of the most important moments in the whole play. On page 57. So I turned to page 57, and discovered that I entered at a moment of high drama. Justin is beating up Priscilla. I come in, and I say: 'I'm sorry, but the Metropolitan Police have a policy of not interfering in domestic squabbles'. (Exits).

I had just about accepted that PC Barr was the best I was going to get, when Gregory said one speech was all I'd have time for, since I'd volunteered to look after the men's wardrobe. Now this was news. Yvonne looked a bit shifty. Said she'd forgotten to mention it. Huh!

If I wasn't keen on that, I was considerably less keen when Gregory asked Yvonne if she was prepared to delve into the inner recesses of her psyche.

'If that's what it takes,' Yvonne said. 'It takes more,' said Gregory. 'It takes energy, teamwork, courage . . . and you have to take your top off in act two, scene two.'

Yvonne said she was up for it.

I certainly wasn't, and I'm not. Yvonne's got an impressive chest, but I don't want her sharing it with the dirty raincoats of Cricklewood. No way. I don't mind ogling Demi Moore or Kim Basinger, but wives shouldn't do that sort of thing.

Gregory wanted to reassure me that the love scene would be amazingly tasteful, discreet lighting and so on. He asked Lance and Yvonne to run it through. Lance immediately removed his vest, to reveal a washboard stomach and no hairs. Bet he shaves his chest. Naturally, I protested. Lance said he was just hot.

He made a ridiculously thespian entrance, said a bit of dialogue, then grabbed Yvonne and applied a major tongue-wrestling hold which she gave every appearance of enjoying. And I thought it was going to be a dry run.

This was too much. I jumped on the stage and pushed them apart.

Yvonne was angry. Lance was amused. Gregory stamped his little foot. And my itching started really badly.

Gregory gave everyone a lecturette about acting and the nature of theatre and illusion tinged with the harshest reality, which was a load of cobblers, and Yvonne and I argued all the way home.

'You've used me for your own naked ambition,' I said. 'And talking of that, I absolutely forbid you to remove any article of clothing in public.'

'If you think I'm going to spoil my big chance, you're even more stupid than I thought,' she said in her gentle, kindly way. 'I'll do whatever the part demands, Gary, and if you cock-up over the outfits, you'll really feel the rough edge of my tongue. And stop bloody scratching.'

There's no persuading her when she's in that mood, so I just went quiet.

JULY

. SATURDAY 1 .

Got Ron to help me on my shopping expedition for the Wildeans. We went to the Stables at Camden Lock, where else? Ron started trying on stuff which made him look like a social deviant, while I attempted to concentrate on a 1950s wardrobe and give Ron the full horror of Friday night. The more I think about it, the more I'm convinced that Gregory is a pervert. If they did the *Sound of Music*, he'd probably have the entire Von Trapp family gyrating topless with tassels on their nipples.

I found a moth-eaten old suit which seemed quite good enough for Lance. The guy on the stall wanted a tenner, which seemed fair. Lance probably won't keep it on for more than five minutes anyway. There was one which looked okay for me. He said he'd take a tenner the pair. Why am I crap at haggling?

I'd been conscious of Frank Sinatra singing 'All The Way' without registering where it was coming from. When Ron wandered over to the next stall, I realized it was an old 78 on a wind-up gramophone. Ron found some old money. The stallholder, a Camden Locky kind of woman who said her name was Ellie, quoted thirty pounds for a vintage fiver. Ron thought I'd be better off getting hold of the banknotes in 1941 and selling them now. A light bulb came on over my head. Bingo! Ron is a genius, and I'll fight any man who says he isn't. Well, argue anyway.

I asked Ellie what was her most valuable 78. She said 'See You Later, Alligator' by Bill Haley and the Comets for £100. And what about war time material? Was that rare? She looked at me as if I was mad. That wasn't stallholder stuff, that was auction stuff. Say a couple of thousand for a rare waxing?

I went back to the first stall, changed into my Wildeans suit, and headed for the war via the big HMV store in Oxford Street.

When I got to the Royal Oak, Reg was being gloomy about the German advance into Russia, and about his wife making him sleep in the kitchen. I didn't like to ask if someone else had been installed in his bed.

He pulled me a pint, musing what Hitler would do when he got hold of all Russia's oil and wheat. 'Make a victory pancake,' I suggested. Reg failed to laugh, so I tried to let him know as subtly as possible that Hitler had made the biggest mistake of the war by invading Russia. He still didn't get it.

Unlike Reg, Phoebe was happy to see me, though she was a bit gloomy too. Why did we never do exciting things any more? Our last date had been on the roof with the incendiaries. I did an involuntary scratch, and said that had been quite exciting enough. But, as it happened, I had arrived with an invitation. How

The moment when I find a wonderful way of making money: transporting 78s across the space-time continuum

would she like to come to Oxford Street and do some shopping?

I don't think a music shop was what she had in mind, but it made a change from the Royal Oak. We wedged into a booth to listen to Frank Sinatra with the Tommy Dorsey Band; Phoebe was worried about Frank being so skinny. I assured her that he'd fill out.

When I told the assistant I wanted two copies of the record, she said she only had one left. But she could order one if I wanted. I wanted. Pulling out a list I'd researched after a quick CD browse, I sent her off to

the stock-room to check, and said to Phoebe: 'I've asked for two copies of the record because I want you to have one'. She thought that was silly, because she didn't have a gramophone, but she'd like a record anyway to remember me by. I said: 'I'm not going anywhere.' She said: 'You always say that, and it isn't true.' 'Well' I said, 'if I save up, maybe I'll buy you a gramophone in the sales.' 'Maybe you won't have to,' she said, pointing at a poster for a talent competition – first prize a radiogram.

I pleaded secret work, but she insisted that I'd walk it, and secretly I knew she was right. Unfortunately, I had a date with the Wildeans, but I said I'd make it if I could so as not to let her down.

The assistant came back with the records. I gave Phoebe most of them to look after, and took three straight to Ellie. I have never seen a woman look so excited. Well, Yvonne occasionally when I'm particularly on form. She got on her mobile immediately to read the titles out to some specialist contact. While she was waiting for him to come back with prices, she quizzed me about how I'd managed to find a collection of records in mint condition in their original sleeves. 'They look,' she said, 'as if they were bought yesterday!' I said, 'Actually today.' But she didn't believe me. I wonder why? So I told her an aunt had died and I'd found a box of them in her attic. There might even be more.

Ellie came back with an offer of £700 for the three, with her taking a £50 finder's fee. I said: 'I found them.' She said: 'It's a figure of speech.' I said: 'It's a figure of cash, but I won't quibble.' I got her to make the cheque out to Ron, who was suitably impressed.

When I got home, Yvonne was trying on her play outfit and did a Marilyn Monroe impression which I found a bit unnerving. I mean, she's a major pin-up, but you don't expect to find her in a suburban bedroom.

Yvonne managed to inform me that she was wearing stockings. I didn't like that at all – stockings and suspenders and Lance felt like a bad mixture to me. She said: 'I'd better get them off,' and I wondered if that was a promise. To account for my mood, I said: 'I'm happy because I've just got my first pay cheque'. Naturally, she demanded to see it. The amount disappointed her more than somewhat. I explained that I was on commission, a tough world, all right for her in her air-conditioned personnel department, me out there at the sharp end . . . She had no idea what a blow it was for me when I got the boot.

Yvonne said she had every idea, since I never stopped whinging and no, there wasn't time for us to rip off all our clothes and work up a sweat. She'd be late for rehearsals. I said she could go without me, but she persuaded me that I had to be there for my pivotal line. And she would

keep the stockings on when we got back . . . I said I was sorry, but the Metropolitan Police had a policy of not interfering in domestic quarrels. Word perfect!

When we got to the hall, Lance was limbering up in his lycra. It struck me that, since I was the policeman, I should have the truncheon. Gregory was all over Yvonne but seemed surprised to see me. Didn't I know it was a main cast rehearsal? But since I was there, I could make the coffee. I chucked my armful of moth-eaten tat at him. (Gary turns on his heel and exits to where he knows he'll be appreciated!)

There was a bit of unrest when I pushed my way towards the front of the queue outside the Rivoli where I'd spotted Phoebe and Reg. I said: 'They've been holding my place while I gave blood.'

Seeing Reg was a surprise, particularly since he was wearing tails. It suddenly struck me that I'd never given him back the suit he loaned me for that awful dinner at the Savoy, and he'd never mentioned it. Poor old Reg – another casualty of war.

He and Phoebe were having some sort of argument about what Reg was going to do in his act when we got to the front of the queue and met the impresario himself, Mr Sydney Wix, whose name was very prominent on the posters. He was taking the names of the talent, seemed a bit harassed, and had a fag apparently glued to his lower lip because it stayed there when he spoke.

Reg said: 'My name is Police Constable Reg Deadman, but I work as Biffo "You Can't Help Loving Him' Bloggs".' Mr Wix had the air of a man to whom nothing would come as a surprise. He wrote it down.

I said: 'I'm called Gary Sparrow. And, no, I don't do bird impressions. I'm a singer-songwriter.' This seemed to baffle Wix. I explained that I wrote songs and sang them. He managed to get his head around that.

The artistes, as I suppose you'd call us, went to wait in the wings. I took Phoebe with me for moral support. Wix, having unglued his fag, turned out to be quite a good master of ceremonies. The audience seemed to have come to dare people to entertain them, not that the competition was up to much – a tap-dancer who kept falling over, a Tommy Handley impressionist, a little girl with a recitation she couldn't quite remember and who, as a result, burst into tears.

Then it was Reg's turn. Phoebe had tried to warn me about what was to come, but I hadn't grasped the full extent of the horror, until Biffo opened his act with that rib-tickler – 'My dog's got no nose'. Poor Reg. He didn't realize that he needed a straight man for his act. 'My dog's got no nose,' says Reg. Silence. 'My dog's got no nose,' says Reg again. 'And you've got no idea, mate,' shouts a voice from the back. That got a laugh.

Unsettled, Reg moved on to 'My wife went to the West Indies.'

'How does she smell?' shouted the same voice. The audience cracked up. I could see a role for Reg in the present, as a turn with Reeves and Mortimer perhaps, but in 1941, no.

I put my head in my hands when he asked: 'What will Hitler do with Russia's oil and wheat?', and when that fell as flat as a pancake, he whipped out a ukulele, managing only the first line of 'Mr Woo' before he retreated under a hail of vegetables. And I thought there were shortages.

The night I shared my talent with the world

I was next. Wix introduced me as Barry, which didn't help, and my nerves hit air-raid level when I walked out on to the stage and saw all the faces. I'd never confronted an audience before. I tried to turn back to the wings, but my feet wouldn't work. I needed desperately to sit down, and the nearest seat was the piano stool, so I aimed at that. At least I got there without tripping.

Fighting an unbearable urge to scratch, I tried to play the intro to 'All The Way', but I was sweating so much my fingers slipped off the keys. There was a bit of nervous laughter. Perhaps they thought I was a comedy act.

No way! I had a scratch, felt a lot better, took a deep breath and tried again. This time it worked. The notes came out in the right order. The voice was a bit weak to begin with, but when I saw Phoebe and Reg giving me a thumbs up, I found myself doing it properly.

Set 'em up Joe ... yup, it's old blue eyes Sparrow with the real thing and, opposite, the very great Al Bowlly

I couldn't bear to look at the audience, so I looked at Phoebe instead, her beautiful face, her smile willing me to win. I would win! I was going to win for her!

The strange thing was that a movie started playing in my head. I was singing the song and looking at myself singing the song, both at the same time. But I was dressed like Sinatra, the trilby, the loosened tie, the whisky on the bar, the barman polishing glasses, the Nelson Riddle Orchestra swelling up from somewhere out of sight. I was a star!

The audience thought so, too. I was mobbed with autograph hunters after the show and Phoebe was so proud it made me feel even better. She was also very shrewd when Wix offered me a tour of the outer suburbs, beating him up to seven guineas a night, plus a set of tails, cost price.

She's a terror when she gets going. She nagged him about the radiogram, too, which he promised to deliver to the pub.

So now it's hallo Ponders End, north London's answer to Las Vegas! Ponders End, I love you! Everybody say yeah! I can't hear you! Everybody say yeah! Yeah, that's better.

I was still singing 'All The Way' when I got back and told Yvonne I'd won a karaoke competition. She said: 'It probably sounded better with the backing track.'

But she had some great news. It turns out that the suit I bought Lance was infested with fleas. He rushed off the stage, came back ten minutes later smothered in cold cream, and resigned from the Willesden Wildeans on the spot! Which means that tomorrow I audition for the part of Justin.

I'm going to be a star across the space-time continuum!

SATURDAY 15.

What a fortnight! I don't know who I am any more. Sometimes I'm Justin, the playboy film director with the sadistic streak. That's at home. Sometimes I'm the young crooner, caressing the ivories and reducing strong men to tears with the sheer beauty of my voice – a hint of Sinatra, a touch of Nat King Cole, a *soupçon* of Al Bowlly. That's in the Royal Oak. Plus, I'm also the thrusting young businessman, on the verge of pulling off a complicated deal for Ron. Wish I could stop scratching; it's getting a bit manic now.

. M O N D A Y   1 7 .

Went to see Ron to get the story absolutely straight in case Yvonne calls him. If she wants to know, I'm on the verge of clinching a quarter of a million pound contract with Sashimi Oil Plc, meaning I'm going to have to keep flying up and down to Aberdeen at the drop of a hat.

I told Ron that if I pulled it off, it would catapult Nostradamus Printing into the premier division. All I need to do is convince Mr McRae to convince Mr Yakimoto that we can do a better job than the printers in Nagoya. It's going to be hard, but I'm going to do it! For Ron!

Ron reminded me that it was all a lie. I said: 'If I've learned anything from amateur dramatics, it's that you have to believe in what you say. That's the definition of a good actor.' Ron said: 'It's also a good definition of a psychopath, and aren't you overdoing things a bit?'

I told him: 'I've never felt more on top of things, and Yvonne is so proud to have a husband on the verge of clinching a huge deal in the face of vicious multi-national competition. I mean, when I told her the Italians had sunk to the level of bribing Mr McRae with a week in Sorrento, in the company of two ladies of the night, she said it was unbelievable.' Ron said: 'It is unbelievable, because you made it all up.' So?

With the present simmering nicely, I headed back to the past and my opening night at the Rialto, Palmers Green. I've planned a balanced little collection: 'Love Is The Sweetest Thing' in tribute to the wonderful Al Bowlly, then a few of my own songs: 'Yesterday', 'Lady In Red' for Phoebe.

Reg started nagging me to include 'I Love Bananas Because They've Got no Bones', a masterpiece which has hitherto escaped me. One of George's, I believe.

. T U E S D A Y   1 8 .

What a triumph (though I say so myself). They loved me! Cheers, encores . . . In 1941, I'm bigger than Wet Wet Wet. Two hundred people just ate out of my hand!

I was so pleased that I went to see Ron, still in my top hat, white tie and tails which, come to think of it, got a few funny looks on the Metropolitan line. I woke him up, but what the hell? We had to get to Joe Allen's and mingle with the other celebs. I needed to laugh, to talk, to eat, to drink, to air-kiss Lionel Blair and swop anecdotes with Andrew Lloyd Webber.

Ron was a real misery. He insisted on driving me home. So, in the end, I shared my triumph with myself and a glass of whisky in the sitting-room.

I tried to be quiet, but Yvonne woke up, and wanted to know why I

was dressed like a head waiter. I told her she had no idea how formal the Japanese could be, and that things were going really well. There was a nasty moment when I saw Mr McRae had a new Cartier watch, which meant the French had upped their bribes, but I was quietly confident.

Since she was awake, she felt like going over our lines, which was fine with me. I told her that a theatre full of people had reacted to me as if I was the best thing since powdered egg. Amateur dramatics were a doddle in comparison. She didn't get the powdered egg reference and wondered whether I wasn't overdoing things. I told her I'd never felt better.

Plaistow Astoria next – day after tomorrow.

.WEDNESDAY 19.

Skipped down Duckett's Passage and danced up to Phoebe's flat. There was a disgusting smell, which I hoped wasn't lunch, but it turned out to be carpet cleaner.

Phoebe was a bit off-hand. She'd been expecting me to come round after the show. I said: 'I was called in to work for an emergency briefing. With Japanese radio transmissions increasing, it could mean they had designs on French Indochina, thus threatening Malaya and Singapore, not to mention Hawaii and Australasia . . .' Phoebe said it sounded like rubbish, but it calmed her down.

Then Reg and Wixy staggered in with the radiogram, and she was so happy! She'd forgotten all about it. She got out the Sinatra record and gave it to me to put on. Not being used to old technology, I forgot about the need for a needle.

Phoebe and I danced. Wixy said: 'Fred and Ginger can sleep easy in their beds. D'you fancy doing an extra couple of numbers, moving up the bill?' I took it as a tribute to my talent. But it turned out that the fire-eater had gone down with a septic toe. Phoebe said: 'He'll do it for an extra ten bob.' Wixy tried to haggle, but Phoebe was having none of it. She obviously has my career mapped out. Today Plaistow, tomorrow the Palladium! And why not?

Wixy brought me down to earth with a bump. He thinks I'll never mean much as a singer, but if I were to flog my songs, then I'd really make it big.

Danger signals started flashing when he said: 'I'm sure I could sell "With a Little Help From My Friends" to Vera Lynn,' and whipped out a publishing contract he happened to have with him. 'You're not signing anything unless a solicitor looks at it first,' Phoebe said.

'I'm not signing anything at all, period,' I said.

This provoked a rather bizarre interlude, since the phrase was new to them both. I explained that Americans said: 'I'm not doing that, period', for added emphasis. Phoebe thought it was silly. 'Do they say – "Hallo, comma, how are you, question mark?"' she wanted to know. Sometimes she can be so frustrating.

Wixy thought I wasn't signing because he wasn't big-time enough, but I explained I'd had a publishing deal before, in America, and it hadn't worked out. Wixy said: 'It's because the Yanks have no bleeding class.' 'No,' I said, 'it just wasn't compatible with my secret war work. I'm quite happy with my job, doing a few concerts for pin-money, and spending time with Phoebe.'

Phoebe threw a real spanner into the works when she said: 'I don't know if I want to spend time with a no-hoper'. An argument loomed. She chucked Wixy out, then really went for it. When I'd been flitting back and forth to Hollywood, telling her my stories, I'd opened a window on another world for her. Now I was turning my back on that, turning my back on a fortune, on glamour, all of which she wanted to experience with me. Weakly, I mentioned Donald. 'Donald,' she said, 'is out the window.'

She wants more than Donald can give her. And if I refuse to give her what she wants, what kind of husband will I turn out to be? Husband! She told me to think about it. 'Yes, Yvonne,' I said. Oops!

Feel really confused about that. I suppose I haven't really thought a lot about the future with Phoebe. If I have, it's on the basis of things going on more or less as they are, dipping in, dipping out . . . But she obviously has very definite plans. Marriage! Would it be bigamy?

Phoebe was very much on my mind at the Wildeans rehearsal, too much, as it turned out. It was all going quite well, until Yvonne gave a speech that wasn't in the script. It was Yvonne's face, Yvonne's voice, but Phoebe's words.

'I want more than he can give me,' she said. 'But you can give it to me, you know you can. And if you won't, well, what kind of husband are you going to turn out to be?'

I froze, completely and utterly. Had I not noticed the speech before? Was art imitating life? I just stood there, totally paralysed. Gregory threw a wobbler, which steadied me down a bit. The play opens on Saturday, and if I don't get it together, then he'll take over. Yvonne hissed: 'I'm not snogging a man who wears dentures,' and did her speech again. It was quite different this time – what I'd been expecting her to say. So, it *was* just a weird flash after all!

She seems quite worried about me, and thinks I should see a doctor. *Moi?* I'm fine.

.THURSDAY 20.

Went to see the doctor. He's a bit of a joker is Dr Jakowitz. I explained my symptoms – sudden fatigue, inexplicable bursts of *déjà vu*, panic- attacks, manic depression, an unusually high build-up of ear wax . . .

The doctor said: 'I should refer you to a psychiatrist, but since there's a seven-year waiting list, it isn't such a good idea. The only way to become an urgent case it to run amok in Safeway's with a machete.' I asked about pills. He said: 'Running around Safeway's with pills isn't as scary.'

When I told him about the play, he became more sympathetic and wrote me out a prescription. I offered him a couple of tickets. He seemed a bit disappointed when I said the play wasn't on Shaftesbury Avenue. But it was on Broadway . . . Cricklewood Broadway. 'Do you know St Saviour's Church Hall?' I asked. 'Do I look like the sort of man who would know St Saviour's Church Hall?' Dr Jakowitz replied.

If I can just get through the next few days, everything will be fine. Perhaps I have been overdoing it a bit. Wonder what effect the pills are going to have?

.FRIDAY 21.

Hey, great pills! They seem to work fine. Feel very calm, very relaxed. Don't know why I ever worried. I'm going to wow the good dockers of Plaistow?

Oh God, spoke too soon! The theatre was huge! Phoebe took a night off, came along, and was well impressed. Big time! I wasn't sure, myself. Took a pill to calm me down. Then another. I knew that if dockers didn't like you, they didn't hide their feelings, and I said so to Phoebe.

She said: 'If you don't want to perform, why not take up Wixy's publishing offer?' Great! Lots of understanding there.

The first two acts didn't produce too much hostility. Then Wix introduced the comedian going on before me, Phil McCaverty. He'd been dreadful earlier in the tour, but now he was truly appalling. He did the strawberries joke, saying: 'If they hadn't been in the same bed, they wouldn't be in this jam.' He did the elephants removing their trunks to make love under water. And he made the horrible mistake of introducing each joke with 'Here's one you'll like'. They didn't. 'I'm too good for this place,' he said as he passed me in the wings.

Then it was me. I took two pills and put a quivering foot on to the stage. As I did, an air-raid siren went off. Thank you, Goering!

Of course, there wasn't a shelter. Instead we all huddled under the stage, surrounded by old props. Wixy was a happy man – he could keep the takings under his no-refunds policy.

I'd taken a few more pills, and had achieved karmic bliss. I also seemed to be speaking my thoughts, like I should have checked for air-raids before I took the gig. Phoebe thought I meant the pills were called gigs. Wixy said they were obviously effective, so I gave him one. Then Phil took some. The other people took some. I gave Phoebe two, and took the last two myself. What the hell! There were a few explosions up above, but what the hell! Immortal, invincible Gary Sparrow. Do your worst, Herman!

Phil did his worst by telling some more of his crap jokes. I remarked: 'You've been dropped by the Germans to lower morale,' which nearly led to a punch-up. Wixy said: 'Why don't you sing a song.' So I taught them 'I Am The Walrus'. And why not? It took them a while, but they got it.

Don't remember anything else. I woke up in Phoebe's bed, but Phoebe wasn't there. Then she was there, then she wasn't. Reg was there at some point. Then he wasn't. It all seemed quite confusing. When there was nobody there, I got up and wandered about a bit in my white tie and tails, which were rather crumpled. Well, they were a bit filthy, to tell the truth. I knew I was meant to be somewhere, but where? Ron would know, good old Ron, my mate, my buddy.

He was on the phone in his office, obviously talking to Yvonne, because he said 'Yvonne'. The old brain was still working. He threw me into his car and drove me, wittering something about how if I didn't get my act together, Yvonne was chucking me out and where had I been for the past twenty-four hours? I had to tell him the truth. 'Flying,' I said.

He delivered me to the back door of the church hall. Yvonne said: 'You look terrible.' 'I am the Walrus', I told her, sitting down rather heavily. She thought I was ill, Gregory thought I was drunk. Hah! Sod 'em all. Move over Hugh Grant!

People seemed to be helping me change, and other people seemed to be putting make-up on my face. I just wanted to sleep, really. Ron walked me up and down, then took me to the wings.

The curtain rose. There was Dr Jakowitz, good old Dr Jakowitz. Wonder if his first name is Robert? Dr Robert? Yvonne made herself a pretend gin and tonic. Lovely girl, Yvonne. I was thinking about Yvonne, when Gregory shoved me rather hard in the back, and I was on stage with Yvonne. But where was the piano? That bothered me. Plus, I couldn't remember my first number.

Yvonne spoke: 'You may as well admit it,' she said. 'I know you're sleeping with that common little barmaid.'

I passed out.

AUGUST

TUESDAY 8.

Don't want to go through that again. Don't even want to write about it. At least the cover story explained the crack-up. Yvonne thought it was due to working too hard and was full of sympathy. Well, she was full of sympathy at first. Recently she's started nagging me to go back to work, saying: 'How can you spend all day channel-hopping?' And: 'What on earth is interesting about the news on the Spanish channel?' And: 'Do you need to spend so much time reading Ceefax?' Well, yes I do, Yvonne. These things broaden the horizons, keep you up to date. Must see if the chance of rain in London has increased or decreased.

THURSDAY 10.

Yvonne now in full attack mode. I told her this morning I might chance going in to Nostradamus for a couple of hours, just to see how it felt. I thought that 'hang the flags out' was a bit of an unnecessary response. After all, I was genuinely ill. Still don't feel a hundred per cent. What happened to the soup and sympathy? Gone, apparently.

Yvonne's worried about what would happen to us if she couldn't work. I said: 'You're not ill, are you? She said: 'No. I'm late.' I thought she meant late for work, but she meant late. As in period stuff.

She seems a bit uncertain about it all. I guess she's looking to me to be happy, but it's one of those things you never think will happen. And when it happens, it happens.

She's a week-to-ten days late apparently, but I don't understand whether that's really late or just a bit late. What I do know is she's never been this late before.

Help! Must talk to Ron.

Wonder again if talking to Ron is such a good idea. He seemed to think congratulations were in order. I told him I'm petrified. I can't have kids at this stage in my life, not till I decide what to do about Phoebe and sort that situation out. As for Yvonne, our relationship yo-yos about, up one minute, down the next. I admit that some of it's my fault for taking my eye off the ball, but if we have a kid then we're stuck with each other.

And I just don't know about kids anyway. I mean, I'm no good with them. What if it's a girl? If it's a boy, I'd know how to deal with it. I could throw a ball, and it would run after it. Easy. Whatever it is, I'll have to push it on swings and read it stories at bedtime. No more nights at the Royal Oak . . . just endless nappy changing. Nappies! That's disgusting! How do women manage?

Ron doesn't see what the big deal is. He's a pillock.

Just writing this down is making me miserable. Yvonne won't be back for a couple of hours. I wonder if there's time . . . ?

. FRIDAY 11 .

Popped back. Had a nice chat with Reg. Well, a chat. Talked to Phoebe, who seemed a bit nervous. She has to go to Buckinghamshire, which she pronounces Buck-ing-ham-shire, making it sound like Outer Mongolia. I guess it would seem like that to an East London girl – Oxford Street is the farthest she's ever travelled.

She's never told me about her cousins before – evacuees. Their parents were killed in the Blitz.

Being Phoebe, she put a brave face on it, pretended she was looking forward to the countryside. But she's really scared rigid. She suddenly went into a big number about liking streets and brick walls and feeling the pavement under her feet, and how they have animals in the country and bats and owls and things that fly into your hair at night.

I love Phoebe when she's vulnerable. In fact, I love Yvonne when she's vulnerable. Why aren't women vulnerable all the time? Why do they have to push you and shove you and make you feel you're not living up to their expectations?

Phoebe wants me to go with her. We'd be Mr and Mrs Sparrow, all alone in the country air. And she says you can do things in the country that you can't do in London. 'Like what?' I said, acting dumb.

Country air with Phoebe is just what I need to put me right back on my feet. I can tell Yvonne I'm back in harness. That'll cheer her up. Yes, a little trip for Ron, intensive negotiations in Aylesbury. Might even have duck for dinner!

SATURDAY 12

Yvonne came home in a good mood. She's convinced she's pregnant. She wasn't sure about wanting the baby in the morning. She was sure in the afternoon. She wasn't sure on the way home. But now she's thrilled, over the moon, up for it. She thinks it's going to be the making of us, just what our marriage needs. She's going to take a couple of days off to stay with her mum and break the good news gently. She didn't seem too put out when I said I didn't fancy it. She even told me to take a walk in the country. Well, I always do what Yvonne tells me!

MONDAY 14

And it's off to the countryside! Phoebe was really excited and talked nineteen to the dozen all the way down in the train. She didn't seem to notice that I'd gone a bit quiet.

This pregnancy thing is a bit of a problem. If I'm going to be a father, then that's the end of my trips to the past. I'm going to have to live in the present full-time. It takes some thinking about, and it was very much on my mind during the journey.

Why is that when everything seems to be going right, it can suddenly turn so wrong?

Of course, there was no taxi at the station. Of course I did the gentlemanly thing and carried both our cases. Even in wartime, women seem to take vast amounts of stuff on their travels.

Phoebe was a bit freaked out when a cow mooed from behind a hedge. In fact, she jumped several feet into the air. Then she pretended she knew it was a cow all along, she just hadn't expected them to be hiding behind hedges. She's so lovely!

And we walked. And walked, and walked, and walked. I'd brought a map with me, but unfortunately it was a modern map, and nothing seemed to make sense. Phoebe wanted to know what the M25 was. I looked at the beautiful countryside and told her she was better off not knowing.

The sun shone. There was no one about. Phoebe looked beautiful. She turned her face up to me for a kiss. She seemed to want to take things further. And I stopped. I stopped! She couldn't understand why, and I couldn't tell her. I pretended that I didn't want to frighten the cows, and we walked on, me feeling like hell.

After only another hour, we got to the top of a hill and there was the farm. It looked like one of those Victorian pictures you get on yucky greetings cards, only this was real. There were even ducks pottering around a duck pond.

As we walked down the hill, Phoebe warned me again not to say that the kids' parents were dead. She thought it was better for Sally and Peter not to know yet. As far as they were concerned, the parents were away.

So was the farmer, in the army, but his wife looked just like a farmer's wife should – round-faced and rosy-cheeked. Phoebe introduced me as her husband. I confirmed that I was. Mrs French wanted to know how long we'd been married, so we had to have a hurried consultation. I whispered: 'Two years'. Phoebe thought it couldn't be that long. 'Two months?' We agreed on six. Mrs French twinkled a bit, and said however long it was, she had still put us in the big bedroom across the hall.

Then the kids came rampaging in, and I found myself talking to them as if they were adults. It was stupid, but I couldn't think of anything kiddish to say. I felt even worse when a Yank in RAF uniform arrived who

Mr and Mrs Sparrow meet Mrs French and the kids. They also meet
Hero Harry, which isn't such a pleasure

obviously had the gift that I lacked. He did mock boxing with Peter, and called Sally 'Princess'. Great!

The Yank said he was called Harry. Phoebe said she was called Phoebe Bamford – no Sparrow. My wife.

Harry asked what I did.

'Oh,' I said, 'I play the piano a bit, tickle the old ivories . . . How about you?' 'Well,' said Harry, 'I'm flight navigator with one of the bomber crews at the airbase. Just got back from a raid over the Baltic. It was pretty hairy, took a lot of flak, came back on one engine . . . So, what do you play on the piano, then?'

I knew that it was going to be one of those days, particularly when Phoebe looked impressed by Harry's tale. I bet he was making it up! I tried to get her to come upstairs on the pretext of a wash and brush-up. I even said she could watch me shaving, but the prospect didn't grab her.

So I went upstairs. Since I'd mentioned shaving, I thought I might as well shave. I aerosoled myself with foam, wet the razor – still no Phoebe. I went back downstairs.

As I'd suspected, Harry was giving Phoebe some heavy chat. 'Over-paid, over-sexed and over here,' I said. He looked surprised. I realized I was a bit early with that phrase. But he was impressed with the aerosol. One up to Sparrow!

Finally he shoved off, though not before inviting me and my wife to a kids' party at the airbase tomorrow.

Well, what do you do in the country, apart from eat great food that tastes like food should? I'd never really thought about it before.

.TUESDAY 15.

Yvonne and I don't do much country stuff. After the walk from the station, I didn't feel like another one. So I played with the kids a bit, and got more used to them. Phoebe's great. She'd make a lovely mum. Trouble is, I'm going to be a dad back in the present, so I'm a bit confused.

The vicar's magic was nothing compared to the magic of Phoebe and me in the hayloft

I'm still confused, and now I've confused Phoebe. We lay there in our big bed, her waiting for me to make a move, me pretending I had a headache! Pathetic! Then she made a move and I pretended to be asleep. I heard her crying quietly so that I wouldn't notice. But I did. Poor Phoebe. What a mess.

We didn't have time to ourselves until we set off for the airbase. Then Phoebe wanted to know what the matter was. She said she fancied me and she knew I fancied her, she'd felt the proof of that last night. So why didn't I want to, after we'd waited so long for the opportunity? I muttered something limp, feeling anything but, and we went on, not talking.

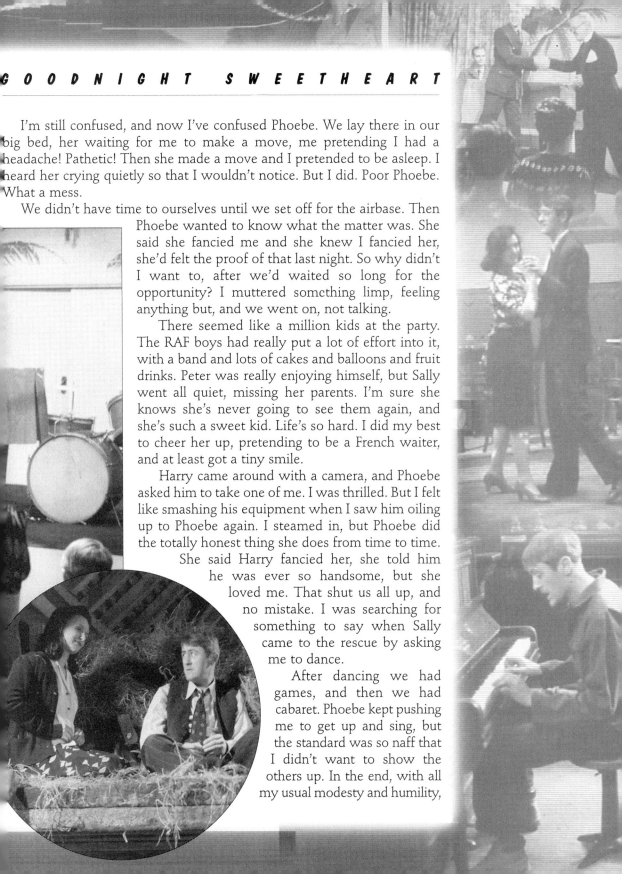

There seemed like a million kids at the party. The RAF boys had really put a lot of effort into it, with a band and lots of cakes and balloons and fruit drinks. Peter was really enjoying himself, but Sally went all quiet, missing her parents. I'm sure she knows she's never going to see them again, and she's such a sweet kid. Life's so hard. I did my best to cheer her up, pretending to be a French waiter, and at least got a tiny smile.

Harry came around with a camera, and Phoebe asked him to take one of me. I was thrilled. But I felt like smashing his equipment when I saw him oiling up to Phoebe again. I steamed in, but Phoebe did the totally honest thing she does from time to time. She said Harry fancied her, she told him he was ever so handsome, but she loved me. That shut us all up, and no mistake. I was searching for something to say when Sally came to the rescue by asking me to dance.

After dancing we had games, and then we had cabaret. Phoebe kept pushing me to get up and sing, but the standard was so naff that I didn't want to show the others up. In the end, with all my usual modesty and humility,

I allowed myself to be dragged to the stage.

I said I'd like to dedicate the song to a very special lady, and would she please join me. Sally looked at Phoebe, but Phoebe knew who I meant, and encouraged Sally to come and sit with me.

I sang 'Here, There and Everywhere', absolutely and totally from the heart. Sally thought it was for her, but Phoebe knew who I was singing for. I sang the song as if I really had written it; every word was true, and every line was about Phoebe and me.

Afterwards we slipped away – there'd be no problem with the kids finding their own way back. We walked hand in hand, heading for a place where we could make our dreams come true.

In the end it was a hayloft, but it felt like the Imperial Suite at the Savoy or a golden beach on a desert island.

Forget the future, forget the past. Phoebe and I were together, truly together, and it was as amazing for both of us as we'd always known it would be. I don't care about anything now. I'll never care about anything again but Phoebe.

WEDNESDAY 16

Yvonne isn't pregnant after all. What a relief! Don't think I'm ready for fatherhood, unless I could bring Sally back with me. If I ever do become a dad, I think I'd like a little girl.

FRIDAY 18

Off to Leipzig for Ron. Actually, back to my rooms with Mrs Bloss. This 78s lark is brilliant. I'm coining it, Yvonne thinks I'm Mr Super Salesman and is really proud of me – life couldn't be better.

Phoebe's just left in a state. Life couldn't be worse. The brewery wants to put a new tenant in, since their agreement was with Eric. I said she had to write a letter, but she wasn't sure what words to use, so I said I'd write one for her and everything will be all right. Must buy an old manual typewriter.

Bloody hell! As one door closes, another one closes. Literally. Walked up Duckett's Passage as usual, and what do I find? A building site! They've started knocking things down in the present. How the hell am I going to come and go now? Fortunately, the building workers seemed as shocked to see me as I was to see them, so I cleared off, sharpish.

The old typewriter is unbelievable! The keys keep sticking. I was wrestling with it when Yvonne came in and turned on the news. There was a story at the end of the local bit about building workers downing tools because a ghost in World War II clothes materialized in their midst, gave them a chorus of 'There'll Be Bluebirds Over The White Cliffs Of Dover', and vanished.

Honestly, the things people make up. But I'm a celebrity! And being a ghost could be helpful.

SATURDAY 19.

Went to recce the building site, and found the workers working. I pretended to be from Health and Safety, wandered around a bit, and found myself in 1941. Bingo! That'll give them something to talk about!

When I got to the Royal Oak, Phoebe was talking to a Trevor Howard look-alike. She introduced him as George Harrison, but I said he couldn't be – his hairstyle wasn't right.

It turns out that George is the area manager for the brewery, the bastard who's trying to chuck Phoebe out, so I handed him the letter. He didn't even bother to read it, just spouted a lot of crap about it being against brewery policy to give a tenancy to a woman, and how he had complete discretion in running his area. I

George Harrison makes anything but sweet music with Phoebe

said this wasn't the spirit of Churchill, and couldn't he use his initiative?

George said he was moved. George said he had an idea. George took Phoebe aside and started whispering to her. I could see her getting more and more angry. Finally she chucked him out.

At first she wouldn't tell me what he said. But it turns out that he'll let her keep the tenancy if he can get his feet under the table and his leg over Phoebe on a regular basis. What a creep! I tried telling her everything would be all right, but I haven't got the faintest idea what to do. Help!

SUNDAY 20.

Good laugh as I was coming back. Some yobs had broken into the building site. I could hear them saying the ghost story was crap. So, as I passed, I said: 'Good evening'. Boy were they scared! It even got on the radio. At this rate I'll be the silly story on News at Ten!

Yvonne and I were having lunch when the phone rang and some rather distraught woman called Mary Cunningham was on the other end, desperate to speak to my wife. Yvonne made not wanting to talk motions, so I told Mary she was out. Mary started sobbing and getting hysterical about Mr Grainger being parked outside her flat watching her.

Turns out she's complaining about being sexually harassed in the office, but Yvonne doesn't believe her. The Grainger bloke is drop-dead gorgeous with thighs like Michelangelo's *David*, to quote Yvonne, and Mary's a mousy typist with a squint.

Now, if I said something like that, I'd be accused of blatant sexism. How do women get away with it?

Yvonne told Mary to come and see her first thing, and we went back to the roast beef and Yorkshire. I explained my theory, that harassment was to do with power rather than sex. Yvonne stood on her professional dignity, wondering why a fully trained personnel person should subscribe to the theories of a failed television repair man. But I did make her think, or at least sowed some doubt, so she thought she'd wire Mary up. That sounded a bit drastic, but it turned out Yvonne meant plant a little tape recorder on her.

I lunged across the table, getting gravy on my sweatshirt, and hugged her. She couldn't understand why. I couldn't explain.

MONDAY 21

Deciding to make the most of my new fame, I strode through the building site in full 1940s gear, with the builders falling back in horror. What a brilliant laugh! I can't wait to tell Ron.

When I got to the Royal Oak, Phoebe was very depressed, talking about joining the WAAFs. I whipped out my little box of tricks, which meant nothing to Phoebe or Reg. 'It's the latest American technology,' I told them, 'top secret.'

If only every case of sexual harassment could be solved by the use of technology

I got Phoebe to say a few words, taped them and played them back. The reaction was as good as the one I got on the building site. Reg examined it closely. His trained eye spotted the line – Made in Japan. I explained that was to throw people off the scent, and that SONY stood for Somewhere Outside New York.

Harrison was due in any moment. Phoebe went to sit at a table, hiding the recorder, and when he arrived Harrison made a bee-line for her. She led him on brilliantly, getting him to say exactly what he had in mind for their little arrangement, the sleaze-bag. If she slept with him, she could keep the tenancy. Then she called me over and gave me the machine. I asked Reg to join us, and played back the tape.

Harrison went white. He tried to deny everything, but what could he say? I ejected the tape, and asked Reg to look after it in his official police capacity.

Harrison was desperate for us not to tell the brewery. I said we'd keep things quiet on condition that Phoebe got the tenancy, and he paid for a couple of barrels of beer a week out of his own pocket.

Well, a hero deserves his reward, and when Phoebe said she was popping upstairs to put the kettle on, I had a feeling that there was more than tea on the agenda . . . I can't understand why we waited so long.

When I left, Reg told me that it was Phoebe's birthday the day after tomorrow. I've got to be there for that, building site or no building site.

Got home at 9.30 p.m., to find Yvonne in bed. Not ill, just fancying an early night with her insightful failed television repair man and full-time genius! It turns out that thunder-thighs Grainger has been making Mary's life hell, the result being that Grainger's been given the boot and Yvonne has been promised a gold star on her next performance review.

Why do I feel I don't deserve two women who are both crazy about me?

.TUESDAY 22.

Woke up in the early hours with a terrifying thought. WHAT'S GOING TO HAPPEN WHEN THEY'VE BUILT WHATEVER THEY'RE BUILDING? HOW AM I GOING TO GET BACK TO PHOEBE?

Wondered how to stop it. Decided to campaign for the preservation of a unique part of the East End. Called on Ron for support. He loves me being the ghost, not so sure about the campaign. Made some placards. Mounted a demo. Nobody interested. What am I going to do? Made a complete prat of myself on a news interview. What am I going to do?

Yvonne saw the interview and made me feel even more of a prat. What am I going to do? They've got security guards on the site now, alsatians, razor wire. It's like a p.o.w. camp. Plus, there's two storeys of Portakabins blocking my way back.

Okay, here are the arguments. My mum always told me if I had a decision to make I should write down the plus points and the minu points, add up each side, then decide.

FOR STAYING IN THE PRESENT	AGAINST STAYING IN THE PRESENT
Yvonne thinks I'm a hero	It won't last
I've got a good business with my 78s	If I can't go back, to buy more, I'll have to get a job
It's not fair on Yvonne to have Phoebe	It's not fair on Phoebe to have Yvonne
I can't hack the past full time	Perhaps I could now that Phoebe and I ... And now that we're really together, wouldn't it be a waste not to go on?
	I can't miss Phoebe's birthday

Well, that seems clear. So make a plan. And the plan is . . . what? The plan is:

- Go to the building site (well done, Gary, good thinking)

- Break in with wire cutters (need Ron to help)

- Do it early morning and hope the guards are asleep (hope, huh!)

- Find the right Portakabin for 1941 (couldn't they signpost it?)

- Bring Phoebe birthday present (what???).

So, I'll break into the site, dodge the security, rampage through the Porta-kabins and jump. Easy! And I'll write down how I did it, if I manage to do it.

Happy Birthday Phoebe! Can't wait to kiss you good morning, sweetheart!